BY WIND

THE WITCHES OF PORTLAND, BOOK 3

T. THORN COYLE

Copyright © 2018
T. Thorn Coyle
PF Publishing

Cover Art and Design © 2018
Lou Harper

Editing:
Dayle Dermatis

ISBN-13: 978-1-946476-07-4

BY WIND

Sometimes the voices in your head are real.

Brenda should be happy. She runs a successful esoteric shop in Portland. She has a great coven and good friends.

But a voice she doesn't recognize has taken up residence in her head. It's not one of her spirit guides. It isn't her matron Goddess. What does this voice want from her?

Then Caroline walks in, beautiful, with a sheet of perfect black hair, and a face that makes Brenda melt.

She's on the run from danger...

This is a standalone book in a linked series.
One of the characters uses they/them pronouns. This is not an editorial mistake.

1

BRENDA

The first pangs of a headache started at the base of Brenda's skull. It felt like pressure, building up inside of her, waiting to burst free. Or crush her in its wake.

Don't be so dramatic, she thought. *It's just a change in barometric pressure or something.*

Except the sky was blue today. There wasn't any storm on the horizon.

As a matter of fact, Brenda *should* feel energized. This was her time of year. It was almost Vernal Equinox, and the moon was waxing toward half. Everything should feel as if it was tipping toward balance, but instead, everything felt wrong.

She needed balance this year, more than ever. Portland did, too, after the scandals that had rocked local government during the fall and winter. Scandals that Arrow and Crescent Coven had been smack in the middle of.

The sun was out, though the cold rains would be back soon, Brenda was sure. But today was one of those rare, perfect, late March days when people pretended it was warm enough to leave their heavy coats at home and venture out only in a sweater or light jacket.

She should have felt awesome. Instead, it took everything she had to pay attention to the customers, and to keep her psychic shields up and at the ready. The headache made both almost impossible.

The Inner Eye was busy for a Wednesday, late morning. Not jammed, but there were several people browsing the books, gems, divination tools, and herbs.

Lead crystals in the windows caught the sunlight and refracted it into tiny rainbows that danced throughout the store. Brenda tried to soothe her jangled nerves and increasing pain by humming along to Loreena McKennitt's voice and harp.

Tempest, her part-time worker and full-time coven sister, walked toward the back room, with a box of books UPS had just delivered. They would need pricing. This month, the back and sides of Tempest's head were shaved, and a straight fall of teal hair fell down around her delicate face.

"Can't we listen to something other than this cater-wauling?"

Tempest was a gifted massage therapist and also a young smart-ass.

"No. The customers like it." Brenda had loved this album since it was new. She didn't care how many years ago that was. It made her feel like her best, most witchy self, even on days like today, when she really wanted to crawl back into bed with an old favorite book, like one of Charles de Lint's.

It was weird that she felt in such need of comfort. She wondered what was coming. What was wrong.

The bells over the door rang, and young Black man, dressed neatly in a red windbreaker, a retro Run-DMC T-shirt and skinny jeans over Chuck Taylor sneakers looked around, and approached the counter.

"Um...do you have any Palo Santo?" he asked.

Brenda smiled. "I do. Just got some in, as a matter of fact."

She scanned the shelves on the wall, behind the counter, eyes searching the large glass jars. "I put it on this shelf just yesterday..." she muttered. "Tempest? Did you move the Palo Santo?"

Tempest came back, sans box of books. "Yes! Sorry! I took it down for another customer this morning, got busy, and forgot to put it back. It's here."

The jar was down at the end of the long glass display counter, tucked behind some other jars that also needed re-shelving. She held it out to Brenda.

:*The wood reveals the seeker's heart. The young man needs not only cleansing, but protection. Care for him well, before the light around him dims.*:

Brenda almost dropped the jar. That was *not* her intuition, her inner psychic voice. That wasn't even one of her usual spirit guides. It was an actual, practically physically audible, voice inside her head. What the...?

"Whoa!" Tempest said, catching hold of the jar again. "I didn't realize you didn't have it yet before I let go. Sorry about that!"

Brenda shook her head. "It's fine. My fault."

Tempest gave her a look, but didn't say a word, just turned to show some Tarot decks to a couple of Goth teens, their already white skin made paler by black lipstick and layers of black eye makeup.

Brenda took a breath, trying to quiet the sudden inner turmoil, and turned to the young man. "Do you know what size stick you need? I can pour some out for you, so you can choose."

He looked slightly uncomfortable. "Um...I'm not sure. I've never bought any before. Someone just told me it was good...."

His voice trailed off, as if he was embarrassed to be talking about it.

Brenda opened the jar and shook out several pieces of the fragrant wood, inhaling the scent. It was one of her favorites. Palo Santo wood was slightly sweet, smelling of frankincense and copal.

"It's good for cleansing," she said, briskly. She found that if customers were ill at ease, it was best to act as though every single thing in the shop was ordinary, as though it could be found anywhere. She dropped her voice then, fingers playing over the pale, jagged sticks, careful to not look at the young man's face. "Some people also use it for various types of healing work. They say it's good for easing certain types of depression and anxiety."

She looked up again, brightening her expression. "So, do any of these sticks appeal?"

He turned each one over, carefully, fingers sliding across the wood. "I don't know. Does it matter?"

He finally looked up at her, and she could see the fear and confusion in his eyes.

"It only matters to you," she said, putting a slight push of power behind her words. "Everything you choose should be because you want it."

He breathed in sharply. Then shook his head. "If only."

"Don't let them do that to you."

"What?" He backed away from the counter.

Damn. She shouldn't have said that. *Don't scare the customers*, Brenda. She could feel Tempest staring at her, likely wondering what the heck was up. Non-consensual psychic reading. Rookie mistake.

She held her hands up, palms out, in a placating gesture.

"I'm sorry. I wasn't fishing around in your brain, I promise. It's just that sometimes I get hits. Psychic information." She'd already messed up by saying something, so might as well say some more. "And it feels like someone is trying to make you feel like nothing you do will help. I don't know who those people are, but I don't think that's true. I think you have a lot to offer. It's all around you. In your aura."

He kept backing up, slowing, almost crashing into a display of crystals and gemstones. Luckily, he caught himself and veered into the aisle.

"I'm sorry," Brenda said. "I didn't mean to scare you."

She held up a stick of Palo Santo, the first one her hand touched. "Let me give this to you. Please."

He shook his head. "No. Thanks." Then turned and left the store. The bells jingled him out the door. Brenda sighed, scooped the blond shards of wood back into the glass jar, and snapped the lid closed.

Then she put it in its place back on the shelf where it belonged. Something buzzed at the back of her brain. That phrase, "Where it belonged." There was something about the young man...as though he was out of place. No. As if part of his soul was out of place.

Well, that happened sometimes. People gave parts of themselves away to others all the time, actually. It was why soul retrieval was necessary. She just didn't like doing it. It made her sad to have to seek out lost shards of soul like that. Even though reunion should have been a happy thing, something was always different when the piece of a soul came home again.

"It's just change, Brenda. Everything goes through it," she said.

"What's that?" Tempest said from right behind her.

Brenda jumped a little. What was *wrong* with her today?

"Sorry. Just talking to myself. Did those girls buy anything?"

Tempest gave her another look. "Yeah. They wanted to look at the Thoth deck, but frankly, they're not ready for the study it requires yet."

"Sometimes that's how we learn, Tempest. You know that."

"Yeah, yeah. I sold them one anyway. But they also wanted Brian Froud's Faerie Oracle. I figured that even though it's not really Tarot, it'll help teach them how to use the cards in general."

Brenda smiled. The Faerie Oracle was a strange deck, and seemed lighthearted at first, but wasn't really, not when you got right down to it. Brian and Wendy Froud were amazing artists, and Brenda knew they had some real magic between them.

"They also took a flier for the pendulum class. Did you miss this?" Tempest asked, holding up a piece of Palo Santo.

"Damn. I guess I did."

Tempest reached for the jar. Brenda stopped her. "No. Clearly we need to burn it in the shop today. Our usual incense isn't clearing the space well enough. The spirits seem to want something different today."

She just hoped that wasn't an omen. She really just wanted to enjoy this spring.

But for now, there was work to do. She bustled over to a white woman wearing blue jeans and a long, burgundy sweater, who had been steadily taking book after book off the shelf, and was now plopped into one of the two damask reading chairs, looking thoroughly confused.

"Were you looking for something in particular?" she asked.

The woman looked up at her, brown eyes stricken, furrows running alongside her mouth and a crease between her eyebrows.

"I need help," she said. "But I just don't know what kind."

And then she burst into tears.

2

CAROLINE

The desert was unforgiving. Harsh. Beautiful. Dry. The variegated shades of sand and rock soothed the eye with shades of tan and ochre.

The Jeep SUV handled well, and was comfortable enough that driving for several hours at a time the way she did on her buying trips was no hardship.

She'd actually grown to enjoy driving. Enjoyed the time spent listening to music, eating snacks, watching towns and cities and wilderness roll by. Enjoyed the time spent alone.

Air-conditioning set just high enough that she wasn't sweating, but not so cold as to make her forget she was in a hot, sere place, she drove. The P!nk album she'd been listening to had ended thirty miles ago and she hadn't clicked on anything else. The hum of the car was enough for her, though Caroline's thoughts had started crowding in again. She wasn't sure if that was good or not, but for now, she let it be.

This stretch of desert was one of Caroline's favorite places. Completely different from her childhood home of Atherton, a wealthy suburb on the edges of Silicon Valley.

She craved something different than that. Craved a space where a person never knew what might happen. A place that wasn't as dangerous as it had been one hundred years ago, but lethal all the same.

Her people weren't the ones who had built the railroads with aching backs and shoulders, heads protected from the all-seeing sun by flat-brimmed felt hats or the woven rice cones from home. The people who had worked alongside natives and people from Africa, all of them indentured in some way or another. All of them with little choice but to keep going toward the promise that life would become better once the railroad got to wherever the tracks were headed.

But she thought about those people, all the same. It was hard not to, looking out at this landscape. Funny, though, she'd never thought of them until she began to feel so trapped herself.

Her people came from Hong Kong, and had always had enough money to not want for much. In the years since her parents' families had emigrated, they'd become pretty wealthy indeed.

She said it didn't matter to her, but supposed that was easy enough to say, wasn't it?

Caroline needed to start thinking about a lot of things she hadn't thought about before. Her life was cracking open around her, and the light piercing through was practically blinding.

What would be revealed once her head cleared, she didn't know. She just knew she needed to keep moving.

The gem show had been successful. She'd found some amazing pieces, some of which she would have kept in the past, setting them up in displays in the home she and her husband had lived in the last ten years. But she really needed the money now, and those key gems and crystals could sustain a significant markup, which would net her far more than the more common stones she bought in bulk to resell to shops and jewelry makers who catered to people who loved rugged things that shone.

She'd been tucking money away for years, into a business account Rafe had no knowledge of, but all of a sudden, the nest egg didn't feel nearly large enough. She was grateful for whatever instinct had caused her to open the account in the first place. Once it had been set up, it was easy enough to keep going.

Caroline had a gift for rocks and gems. She started off by collecting bits of rock polished by sand and ocean, mixing them with mottled beach glass shards in green and amber and the rarer shards of blue.

She saw things in stones that others often missed. It was what made her such a good picker, and had enabled her to build this business that her husband used to encourage, and now called "your addiction to sparkly shit and wish fulfillment."

He didn't know just how much money she'd made the last few years. That was deliberate. She let him think it had remained a harmless hobby, something nice to make her feel like she was doing something with her time, and contributing a little to the household budget.

It was such bullshit. The only things Rafe respected anymore were razor-sharp intellects, pixels, and money. Caroline was smart, but not in a way Rafe understood. And money? Raised by affluent parents, she had always taken it for granted. Her mouth twisted at that. She popped the lid up on her sports bottle and took a long drink of water.

It wasn't something she was proud of, her disregard for how things worked in the world, but it was just the way her life had been. Rafe had always scrambled for money. He had needed that brain of his to set him free from poverty.

Where she had been free to pursue her passions, Rafe had to be passionate in order to pursue *anything.*

Caroline felt the difference now. She felt it in the sharpness of her hipbones and the planes of her face, slowly revealed as the roundness slid from her muscles and bones. Even her hair, once thick and dark, had started falling out.

But all of that was going to change. Being in hall after hall of gemstones had cleared her confusion. She had invested in some healing gems this trip. Those she would keep for herself.

Mostly, though? Her healing process was kicking itself off with one huge realization: Rafe was a miserable asshole, and she wasn't going back.

Her parents had warned her that he was an unhappy man, though she couldn't see it, early on. Over the years she had explained it away as "Just the way he is. Melancholic." But then he had grown angry. She thought it would pass.

Caroline hadn't realized until recently just how unhappy he would try to make her, too.

It had started off in subtle ways. Undermining her ideas. Mocking her gifts. Then he started escalating. He held her against the wall during an argument, refusing to let her go until she looked at him.

She hadn't wanted to look at him. She didn't like what she saw anymore.

That encounter had left bruises on her upper arms. Other bruises followed.

Oh, he never actually *hit* her, but he started to control her in other ways.

The night before this trip, he had smashed her prized amethyst cluster with a hammer. It had been waiting for her when she got home from a small gem show in the Monterey Bay. The purple crystal tips were left in tiny shards, scattered across her workroom floor. The overhead light had shown the carnage. It was all that she could see, her body rigid, the handle of her rolling gem case still clutched in her right hand.

Rafe had come up behind her then, and touched her. She could feel his fingertips resting lightly on the tops of her shoulders. He leaned his head in close, and kissed her ear, then murmured, "I'm so sorry, babe. I just got so mad at you. I'll buy you a new one."

Caroline forced herself to stand still. She forced steel into her legs and arms and felt it locking up her spine. Then she forced the words out from between her lips. "It's fine. Really. Don't worry about it. I understand."

Because she did. She finally did. She understood exactly what was going on.

She felt him relax and move away. She waited until she heard his footsteps walking down the hall. She waited until she heard the clink of ice cubes in a whiskey glass. She waited until she heard the television click on and the sound of football from the den.

Caroline uncurled her fingers from the handle of the rolling case and went to the kitchen to get the broom.

She had been able to save only one amethyst tip from what had been a massive piece. One of her tasks at the Vegas Gem Show was to have her favorite jewelry worker turn it into a pendant for her. The purple crystal rested just beneath her collarbone now, pointing down toward her heart.

There would be some new punishment waiting for her when she got back home to Palo Alto, she felt that for the truth it was.

Caroline didn't know exactly what she was going to do about it. She didn't know where she was going, or how the hell she was going to get out of that marriage intact.

She just knew it wasn't home anymore. That it never had been. Maybe she would move here, or to some other desert place.

Her cell phone rang from her purse on the car seat next to her. She fumbled into her bag, and checked the number.

It was Rafe. He'd want to know exactly where she was, so he could time her arrival. If anything happened, she would be expected to check and update him.

She clicked "answer" and held the phone up to her ear. The highway was deserted, no cops to give her a talking-while-driving ticket.

"Hey," she said. "The show was great. Yeah. But I set up some meetings with a few shops and vendors that need to happen after the show closes...."

The desert sped by the car windows. The sun was warm on her thighs. The crystal on her breastbone felt solid and good.

"No. I know I didn't tell you. I didn't know until...no. They only got back to me today. Yes, it's important. I'll be here at least another couple of days."

Yeah. He was angry. She could hear it in his voice, though he pretended he was being reasonable. She tried to keep her own voice loose, light. If she grew impatient, or pleaded too much, he would know something was up.

Habit. When did that all become a habit?

"I'll call you when it's all set up. I bet I'll be home on Thursday. Friday at the latest."

It was Monday. That would give Caroline enough time to figure out what the hell she was going to do.

3

BRENDA

Loreena McKennitt had been replaced by the warm voice of Sharon Knight, singing about selkies and sirens, accompanied by guitar, mandolin, and drums.

Brenda's headache was not receding, and now she had to deal with a customer crying on one of the reading chairs in the book section. She sighed, and hoped no one noticed.

Days in the shop sometimes ran toward the strange, and she rolled with it like the professional she was. But today? Brenda just wanted to go home, crawl into bed, and pull the covers over her head.

:There is nothing for her anymore. That's what she thinks, that's what she feels. That is what she is making real.:

It was the Voice again. Brenda tried to keep her hands from shaking, but she wasn't doing a very good job of it. What in Diana's name was going on? She spared a thought to her matron Goddess, the matron of Arrow and Crescent coven, but got no clear response, just a sense of "This one's on you."

Great. She knew the Gods had their own agendas and

weren't at her beck and call, but sometimes, dammit, Brenda wanted guidance.

And occasionally? She had to admit she didn't want the burden of figuring things out on her own. Most times she was good at claiming her own autonomy. It was a big part of her philosophy, and the core of what she tried to pass on to others, both in her classes and in the psychic readings she offered to the community. As a matter of fact, Brenda would have told anyone who walked through Inner Eye's door that she had clawed her way into a sense of sovereignty, bit by bit, and was proud of it. Brenda was unshakeable in her sense of self.

At least, she'd thought she was.

She took in a breath, making sure to fill up from the bottom of her lungs to the top. Then she checked her energy fields. Was anything awry? Her aura seemed cohesive, the the ætheric body closest to her skin seemed a bit jumpy. Agitated.

Brenda imagined her exhalation sending golden yellow light throughout her energy fields. She would need to do some serious work tonight if this kept up, but for now, she would rely on the tried and true practices she did every single day.

Thank the Gods for her spiritual practice. At least that was still a solid thing.

She crouched next to the woman's chair, then reached for the box of tissues Tempest had set out on the low, round table where the woman had stacked entirely too many books.

Tempest always knew when and where something was going to be needed. That was likely why she hadn't put the Palo Santo jar away.

Brenda held out the tissue box, waiting for the woman to

take a few, then asked, "Why do you need help? Are you dealing with grief? Are you in trouble? What's going on?"

Brenda knew in a flash that grief was not this woman's problem, but she had to cover all the bases. Running a successful metaphysical shop seemed to require one-third business, one-third magic, and one-third therapy.

The woman blew her nose until it was red, but the tears stopped, at least.

"They keep telling me to kill myself."

"Who keeps telling you?"

The woman shrugged, and her eyes filled up again. Damn it.

"I'm not sure. So I was looking..." She gestured to the piles of books. Brenda looked at the covers. There were several books on psychic phenomena. Ghosts. Hauntings. And two books on Goetia, which Brenda kept thinking she needed to put in a locked cabinet behind the counter, so only those who were ready, or already knew what they were doing, could get at them.

Strangely, at the top of the stack, was a book on angels. Maybe the woman's subconscious was seeking out her own helpers. The thought of angels was a big comfort to some people.

:*You, too.*:

Her too? Brenda was a *witch*. She didn't mind that other people worked with angels, but they'd never really been her bag. Give her dark nights, a full moon, and a roaring fire, and Brenda was the happiest person on earth. Sure, spirits existed, that was obvious, and other beings, too, but despite being psychic, Brenda had always loved tangible things the most.

Brenda stood and looked around the shop. Tempest helped a man in the back corner, measuring out some dried herbs. Another woman, middle-aged, with curly blond hair, ran her hands just over the small boxes of tumbled gemstones. She plucked one from a box with long, white fingers, and slipped it in the pocket of the red-and-black sweater coat that swung around her hips.

"Excuse me for a moment. I'll be right back."

Brenda swiftly crossed the store, skirts swirling around her ankles, until she was right behind the thief.

"You should know better than to steal from witches," she said.

The woman jumped and turned. "What? What are you talking about?"

Her lips were painted red, the lipstick bleeding into the fine cracks around her mouth. Her dark eyes darted from Brenda's face to the door. They were ringed in brown liner and shadow. It just made Brenda feel sad all of a sudden. And a little bit tired.

"You'd be a beautiful woman if you loved yourself more."

What was *wrong* with her today? That was just rude. All sorts of things were popping out of her mouth. If she were one of her students, she would give herself a time out from doing readings for a month.

The woman's face hardened. "You'd be a beautiful woman if you weren't such a bitch."

Brenda just held out a hand.

"What?"

"I want the stone back." She paused, and sent her awareness outward. "And the jet pendant. And the pendulum. And anything else you have in those pockets of yours."

The woman shoved past her. Brenda put a hand on her shoulder. "Don't."

"Or what?"

She could smell the woman's fear now. Acrid. Bitter.

:Her daughter.: Brenda waited, but the Voice didn't offer anything else. All the same, she gentled her voice. Called on some compassion.

"Whatever you think you need, this isn't it. And this shop has ways of protecting itself that you just don't want to encounter once you've walked outside that door."

"And if I *was* stealing?"

"Empty your pockets, and I'll let you walk away."

The woman's shoulders slumped. Her long white fingers dipped into her pockets, and one by one, she drew the small objects out.

Brenda heard the bells over the door jangle, but didn't turn to see who had come in. Tempest could deal with the new customer.

"Is that it?"

"You tell me."

It was. Well, with the exception of a small bead of hematite. The stone was cheap enough to let go of, and the woman could use the grounding. Speaking of...

Brenda plucked a tumbled piece of rose quartz from one of the boxes and closed her palm around it, whispering a blessing.

"Hold out your hand," she said.

"What?"

"Hold your hand out."

The woman was so startled, she did. Brenda dropped the rosy-colored stone into her palm. "This might help with whatever heart-healing you're seeking. It might help your daughter, too."

The woman gasped, and flung the stone back at her.

"I don't want it."

Brenda stood aside so the woman could pass her, and followed her to the door.

"Well, I hope you find whatever it is you're seeking, then," she said. "And please never come back here again."

Shutting the door, she let the sound of the bells clear her aura, and went to the counter to re-ignite the stick of Palo Santo. Tempest and the young man had both been onto something; the sweet smoke from that wood was needed today.

Shit. She'd forgotten about the crying woman. Maybe the woman could use some Palo Santo, too. Holding a lighter to the tapered end of the piece of wood, she waited until it glowed red and smoke began to curl up around her head in wisps.

Finally, she looked over to the reading nook. The woman was gone. The piles of books had tipped over, and slid across the small table.

Brenda walked over to look, and stifled a curse. One of the books had been left open, face down. A sure way to crack the spine.

It was the book on Goetia.

The woman had been reading about demons and likely scared herself.

"Oh, you poor fool. I hope you find what you're looking for, too. And I hope you come back and let us help you."

:*Too late for that one, I'm afraid.*: The Voice sounded sad. Regretful.

"Why is it you didn't tell me that before? And who are you, anyway?"

The Voice was quiet.

Brenda's stomach muscles clenched and her skin felt a little clammy. A wave of nausea swept through her, and her skin flashed hot, then cold.

She sat down, hard, in the abandoned damask chair, laid her head against the back, and closed her eyes.

The shop bells rang again. She really should get up and help Tempest, but she couldn't quite leave the chair to do it.

Brenda felt someone sit in the chair across from her. Then smelled coconut oil. Tempest. She used the oil in her massage practice and the scent always permeated her skin.

"Brenda? You okay?" The healer's voice was tentative. Soft.

"Are there customers?"

"No. Everyone's gone."

Brenda sighed. "I don't feel very well. Maybe I'm getting sick?"

"You look a little feverish and green. Would you like me to make you up a tisane?"

Finally, Brenda opened her eyes. Tempest's face was neutral, but Brenda could tell she was concerned all the same, just because she knew her so well.

She blinked in the sunlight, which now felt too harsh, almost blinding.

"I think I need to go home. Can you manage?"

Tempest helped her up out of the chair. "Of course I can, but you're not driving yourself home. I'm calling a car for you."

Brenda didn't even argue. She just walked slowly to the back to get her purse.

So much for the beautiful spring day. She hated getting the flu.

She also hoped that was all that was going on.

4

CAROLINE

She pulled into Reno. It had been a long, seven-hour drive, but that had also been just the thing she needed.

Caroline needed to be alone for awhile. To not have other people's opinions crowding her. She needed to figure out what she wanted.

Besides, she *liked* Reno, and some of her favorite shops were there. She planned to find a room for the night, take herself out for a good dinner, and visit shops in the morning. Shop visits were one thing Caroline wished she could do more of, but they only happened en route home from a gem show.

Rafe didn't like her out on the road too much. "You never know what might happen to you."

She could separate out some stock in her room that night, and hopefully leave Reno having made back some of what she spent in Vegas. If she picked just the right pieces, she might even make back most of it.

A woman could dream, right?

Her phone buzzed again. Rafe.

"Shit." She had really hoped he wouldn't bug her for a

day or two, but that had just been dreaming, too. Navigating herself into the hotel parking lot, she found a spot and parked, quickly answering the phone before it went to voicemail.

Rafe hated it when she didn't pick up.

"Hi there! Yeah, I'm just heading out to dinner with some of the dealers. What's up?"

The lie came fairly easily.

She looked across the parking lot at the Spanish-style building of her favorite boutique hotel. It was smaller and quieter than most of Reno's places, a little out of the way, and on the expensive side. Caroline supposed she was going to have to start thinking about saving money soon, but tonight she wanted something nice. Comfortable. Familiar.

Wanting nothing more than to walk past the fountain in the courtyard, ask for a bellhop with a luggage cart so she could empty out her car and get checked in, she forced herself back to the phone. And Rafe.

She reached over to get her sunglasses case from her purse and froze.

"What do you mean?" Slowly, she snapped the case open, put her glasses in the open case, and snapped it shut again. "Why would I lie to you?"

Sweat popped up on her forehead. Caroline's breath was coming faster. She fought to slow it down.

"What do you mean you put a tracker on my fucking car?"

Mistakemistakemistake.

And Caroline separated into two people.

Part of her was in a panic. She never cursed at her husband. She never did anything that might make him angry. Not on purpose.

Neverneverneverneverneverr.

The other part of her looked on with a sense of detachment, incredulous at the stupid game. A game that was dangerous only to her. To her life. To her body. To her soul.

That part of her slammed the Jeep's door open and crouched down. Where would it be? Someplace not to hard to reach. Someplace you could slap it on quickly, and walk away.

"I don't think so," she said as she stood and walked around the front of the car to crouch again. What exactly was she looking for? Something small. Something that looked like it didn't belong.

"What exactly do you *think* I'm doing? So what? So I decided to stop and spend a few days checking in on some of my best customers on the way home and didn't want to freak you out. You know you never let me stay anywhere more than…"

The panicking part had taken the back seat and all the years of anger had moved to the front. Good.

"No, Rafe." She still hadn't found it. Where the hell had he put it? "I have a business to run, and you don't seem able to understand that. No, I'm not talking back to you. I'm just trying to get you to understand."

It didn't seem to be around the front of the car. She headed towards the back, squeezing between a Range Rover and the Jeep. Squatting down again, her eyes scanned under the bumper. Not there. Still holding the phone up to her ear, she got down on her knees and craned her head and neck, trying to look under the car. She was going to have to get all the way down. She stifled a sigh, and half lay, half crouched, on the dirty tarmac. If she were Rafe, where would she have put…

She raised herself back up into a squat. "Rafe, I really don't want to have this conversation with you right now. You know what? I think I never want to have this conversation with you again."

She clicked her phone off, and put her head in her right hand, still leaning on her knees, squatting on the tarmac. A car slowed down behind her.

"Your car okay, lady? You need some help?"

Caroline half turned and waved her hand. "No, just dropped my keys. I'm fine. Thanks for stopping, though."

Rafe would make her pay for this. But she'd had enough.

And she thought she knew just where he planted the device. The bastard had acted all concerned about her tires before she left. She'd thought that was strange, but just shrugged and kept packing the car. She'd wanted to get out of there, and never knew what the heck was going on in his mind anyway. He wanted to play the dutiful husband all of a sudden? Just let him. She couldn't wait to kiss him goodbye and get the hell on the road.

Caroline grabbed the keys from the ignition and jogged back around to the rear. Heart pounding, keys rattling in her shaking fingers, she undid the lock on the spare. Lifting the cover off, she swung it to one side and looked.

"Damn you Rafe," she said. Because there it was, a tiny black box, affixed to the hub of the wheel.

Her phone buzzed in her hand. She ignored it, shoving it into the pocket of her jeans. Well, so much for her plan. There was no checking in to her favorite hotel tonight, no nice dinner. She wasn't even going to be able to see her customers tomorrow. That sucked.

Caroline threw the bug onto the tarmac, and smashed it with the heel of her boot. She'd taken to wearing cowboy boots the past couple of years. She never knew they'd come in so handy. Slamming the tire cover shut, she relocked it, then hurried back around and slid into the driver's seat.

"Looks like we're back on the road, Caroline," she said. But where the hell was she going to go?

She had a friend in Portland, Oregon, who'd been asking her to visit for years. Caroline never had. Rafe had never wanted her to go. For some reason, the short business trips were okay. At least they used to be. But a visit to old friends? There was always some reason for why it shouldn't happen. Never an outright refusal, just a litany of half-passable excuses.

She hadn't even noticed until recently, and by then the pattern was set. It had all felt as if it were too late.

Well, Caroline was burning some bridges now, wasn't she? Might as well see if she could build some new ones.

She backed out of her spot, swung back onto the highway, and headed north.

5

BRENDA

She didn't feel any better, but she wasn't feeling any worse, either. Brenda blinked up at the goldenrod bedroom ceiling and took an inventory. Her head still ached. Her skin felt tight. She rotated her neck from side to side, and rotated her ankles and wrists.

Damn. *Everything* ached. It *almost* felt as though she had a fever, but not quite. She reached toward the bedside table and grabbed her phone. Eight in the morning. Long past her usual rising time. She should feel better after twelve hours sleep, even if they were fitful and plagued with strange dreams.

She really needed to get out of bed and get ready to open the shop. But what *were* those dreams? Brenda slowed her breathing down and tried to relax. Tried to cast her thoughts back to the hazy place between sleep and waking.

But no. The dreams were gone. All that remained was the slightly disturbing sense of them.

"Okay. If we're getting up, we'd best do it now." Groaning, she flipped off the purple-and-orange paisley comforter and swung her legs over the edge of the bed. Oh yeah. Sitting up. She remembered how to do that.

And there was her bedroom altar, with her favorite statue of Diana, hounds at her heels and bow and arrow pointed toward the sky. "Good morning, Huntress."

Brenda paused for a moment, just to center herself. But centering didn't come easily today. She breathed a quick prayer and grabbed her teal velveteen bathrobe from the foot of the bed.

No morning meditation today. No yoga, either. If she did any inversions, she might fall to the rug and never get up again.

"Whatever this illness is, I'm not in favor of it, and would like to lodge a complaint," she said to the bedroom walls. Nothing answered, so she slipped her arms to her bathrobe, opened her bedroom door, and shuffled in her slippers down to the kitchen, tying her robe as she went.

Sun streamed in through the kitchen windows. She loved this room. She loved the antique-red cabinets, the marble-tiled floors, and the white marble countertops. She had spent a lot of money on it a few years ago, knowing it would last for a long time. And knowing that she loved nothing more than having friends over for dinner.

Funny, she hadn't done that much lately. Things were so busy at the Inner Eye all of the time. She paused on her way to the electric kettle, and looked around. How had she let the winter get away without throwing her usual series of dinner parties and gatherings?

Other than Arrow and Crescent coven meetings, she'd barely seen any of her friends in recent months.

She resumed her walk to the tea preparation station on the counter. Filling the stainless steel electric kettle at the deep farmhouse sink, she looked out the window. The hydrangea bushes were blooming purple and blue. The vegetable beds needed some attention. A jay screamed at a squirrel from the Japanese Maple in the corner. The squirrel looked unconcerned.

She flipped the kettle on and got her favorite purple mug out from the cabinet. A black silhouette of a witch on a broomstick flew around the mug; it was thick and heavy, and the handle just fit her.

Brenda still had that queasy feeling. She wondered if she should forgo her usual English Breakfast tea and brew up some fresh spearmint instead. No, she shook her head. She wanted her morning ritual, and she wanted it now.

And then she remembered why she hadn't thrown her usual round of dinner parties. The coven had extra meeting after extra meeting this year, with too many emergencies to deal with, magical and otherwise. First there were the ghosts and the fires, and then the fight with the Interfaith Council, and then, Holy Mother, facing down the police. She shook her head again.

Brenda had never expected ten years ago that she would've ended up embroiled in politics.

"My teachers always told me you never know where the spirit might lead. I guess they were right."

A glimmer caught at the corner of her eyes. Brenda whipped her head towards the door. There was nothing there.

"I really need for whatever this weird stuff is that's happening to go away."

She looked at the clock over the stove. She really had to get a move on. The shop wasn't going to open itself. But really? All she wanted to do was crawl back into bed.

The kettle pinged, indicating that the water had boiled. She poured some over a teabag and set it aside to steep.

Brenda really did wonder if she was coming down with something. The twelve hours of sleep had left her feeling achy and confused. Maybe some honey would ease her stomach. She stirred in half a teaspoon and then turned to get some milk from the refrigerator.

Then she stopped, dead cold, arrested by a shaft of light that shouldn't have been there. She turned to the kitchen windows, and sure enough, the sun was slanting the opposite direction across the countertops.

She looked back. The shaft of light was still there. "No. Please. I just need a normal day."

If she'd been feeling any better, she would've laughed at herself. What was a normal day for a psychic and a witch? She just wanted normal for *her*. Not whatever this new crop of manifestations were: the voice she didn't recognize, the weird dreams, and now the shaft of light in her kitchen.

"Why me? And why now?"

Two days in a row and things were coming out of her mouth that she would've chastised any student or mentee for. She knew the answers. Well, not the *answers*. But she knew those were exactly the wrong questions to be asking. It was never "Why me, why now?" The question a witch would ask was always, "What do I need to pay attention to?"

"Okay Brenda. Get the milk out, make your tea, and get your ass into the shower. Then get dressed, and get to the shop. We can deal with all this weirdness later."

She made her tea with a determination that was almost comical. She would turn the strange state ordinary by sheer dint of her will. And then she turned again, and between her and the doorway to her bedroom was still that shaft of light. She was going to have to pass through it in order to get her day started.

"I don't know who you are, or what you want from me, but you're not going to stop me from going about my day."

Brenda spared a moment to take a deep breath and adjust her energy fields. She made sure that her ætheric body was solid and stable, and then checked the edges of her aura. "This is so strange. I seem fine. Except for feeling like garbage and the fact that there's a shaft of light in my kitchen that shouldn't be there."

Oh well, shaft of light or no shaft of light, voices or no voices, she was going to her bedroom and she was going to take a shower. She took a few sips of tea, clutched her mug to her chest, and plunged through the light.

Then she ran straight to the bathroom and threw up.

"Oh my Goddess," she said, when the heaving finally stopped. "What *was* that?"

A wash of milky tea spread across the black-and-white subway-tiled floor, inching its way toward the teal bathmat, her purple mug tipped on its side. At least it wasn't broken.

She hoisted herself up to the sink to rinse her mouth and splash cold water on her face. Looking at her reflection in the mirror, she barely recognized herself. The face peering back at her wasn't the witchy, early-middle-aged, yoga-going, psychic-reading-giving woman she was so familiar with. Not even a sick version of that person.

No. This person looked...luminous. God-touched. Slightly feverish, but radiant with it.

"I don't understand," she whispered. "What is happening to me?"

The reflection had no answer.

6

CAROLINE

After she left Reno, her phone had buzzed in her purse once every half hour.

Caroline ignored it. She cranked up some music and just kept driving. At one of her breaks, she phoned ahead to make sure her friend Sydney still wanted to see her after all these years, and to ask whether or not she had a place Caroline could sleep.

She'd slept very little, stopping for a couple of hours at a rest stop, and finally, when she just needed a bed, any bed, pulling in to a motel off the highway. She slept for six hours after turning her phone off. The sheets were scratchy and there were rust stains in the shower, but the sleep had been delicious. So had the food in the diner down the street.

After that, she had powered her phone down and just drove straight through. With no phone, she had no GPS, so she just followed what seemed like a sensible route, always adjusting her course north.

It was late afternoon by the time she reached Portland. She felt pretty good, considering the stress of the whole situation on top of the nine-hour drive from Reno. The forests were beautiful. She'd thought about stopping off to see Crater Lake, but had simply greeted the cinder cone as she drove on through.

The San Francisco Bay Area was a beautiful place, but it had nothing on this. Freeways surrounded by swathes of green. Mountains. Volcanoes. And amazingly, blue sky streaked with white clouds.

She had no idea what neighborhood Sydney lived in. She'd said it was in the Rose Park, or Rose City district, wherever that was. "Near the Hollywood Theater," Sydney had said.

Northeast somewhere? But how far east? Might as well just drive through the city until there was a good place to stop for dinner. Sydney had been terribly apologetic. She had a meeting after work that was going to run late and wouldn't be home until close to eight.

Two of the shops Caroline supplied regularly were in the same neighborhood as one another; at least, she thought so. She pulled over, checked her phone, saw the fifteen missed calls and a series of messages from Rafe, and immediately opened up a search engine.

Yes. There they were. The Inner Eye and...The Road Home.

She opened up maps and saw that both shops were within five blocks of each other, one on and one just off Hawthorne.

Perfect. She could eat something, wander around, maybe say hello and see if she could get some appointments to show her stock in person. For years, people had told her that in-person sales visits were the way to go, but she just couldn't do it. The buying trips to gem shows were about all the time she could reasonably spend away from home.

Or, at least, that was what Rafe had said. "Online is the way to go, babe. Why would you want to schlep a bunch of rocks around the country yourself when you can just ship them?"

It all sounded so reasonable. Like everything he said.

She wound the Jeep around some residential blocks, window down, breathing in the jasmine- and coffee-scented air, admiring the old Craftsmen homes and the wild gardens, before finally spotting a parking place large enough for the SUV.

Once the car stopped moving, Caroline let out a breath she hadn't even realized she'd been holding.

"Okay. We're here. We're safe. Let's go get some food."

She wasn't sure whom exactly she was addressing, but it felt good to say those words out loud. She grabbed her big blue purse, swung her legs out of the car, and found herself standing on a Portland, Oregon, street for the first time in her life.

So why did it feel so much like home? She skirted around the Jeep to the sidewalk and looked up into a canopy of maple and elm. Every garden overflowed with a crazy quilt of color and scent. Roses. Hydrangeas. Daffodils. Early vegetables.

Caroline felt like weeping. There was something here that promised nourishment in a way the streets of Silicon Valley never did. Or maybe she was just exhausted.

She wiped the back of her hand across her face and headed to the main drag just up ahead, figuring she'd eat something and then explore the shops.

Turning the corner, she saw a riot of rainbow light. The sign above the shop windows read "The Inner Eye."

"Well, I guess I'm stopping here first, then," she murmured. No GPS, just serendipity and grace.

Bells jangled softly as she opened the door. The air was slightly sweet, but woodsy. It felt calm in here.

"Let me know if I can help you find anything," a woman's voice said.

"Oh!" Caroline startled, and realized she was still blocking the doorway. She stepped further in, looking around. Bookshelves. A reading nook. Tall shelves behind a long glass counter holding jars of what looked like dried flowers and herbs. Tarot cards. And there. A display of crystal orbs and amethyst clusters. Tourmaline. Jet. Raw ruby and opal. Chalcedony. Her fingers itched to touch the stones. She always responded that way.

A younger woman with a long fall of teal hair tucked behind one ear approached her.

"Feel free to pick them up."

"Thank you." She ran her hands over one of the rubies, then held it up to the sun coming in through one of the big plate glass windows. It caught, and a flash of deep, wine red showed itself through the mottled, rusty exterior. "Beautiful."

Caroline liked this place a lot. It was the sort of place she had always wished for as a teen in sterile, stately Atherton. The closest places like it were all the way up in San Francisco, and her parents never liked her going up there with her friends.

Of course, they did it anyway, without telling anyone. But Caroline had the courage to only make that trip twice. Attracted as she was to the crystals, and the classes on auras and herbalism, the pull wasn't as strong as her wish to stay remain in her parent's good graces.

The young woman had gone back behind the counter and was pricing a variety of pendulums. Turned wood. Brass. Rose quartz...

"I'm actually one of your distributors," Caroline said. "Some of these stones likely came from me."

The woman looked up. "Oh? Which company?"

"Amethyst Gems."

The woman's face brightened. "That's great. Your stuff is always high quality. Did you bring any stock with you?"

Caroline grinned for the first time since leaving Nevada. "I've got a whole car full. Just came from the Vegas show."

The woman went to a navy curtain bordered with Celtic knot work. She poked her head through. "Hey, Brenda, Amethyst Gems is here!"

Caroline heard a voice respond, low and soothing.

"You should go on back. Brenda would love to meet you, but she's in semi-quarantine. My name's Tempest, by the way."

Caroline held out her hand. "Caroline." Then she stepped through the open wedge between the curtain and the doorframe that Tempest held open with her hand.

Sitting in the room was an angel.

Caroline gave a small gasp and blinked. Then she saw that the person sitting behind the long wooden table was just a woman with wavy, brown, shoulder-length hair, a flowing green knit tunic, and a gorgeous moonstone pendant nestled on her breastbone.

Caroline reached up and wrapped a hand around her amethyst point, then realized she hadn't spoken yet, and was likely staring.

"Hi! I'm sorry, that moonstone is so beautiful, I think it caught me for a moment."

The woman smiled, and Caroline wished she would smile at her forever. "It has that effect on people sometimes. It was my mother's, and it's one of my greatest treasures."

She gestured to a chair. "Please, have a seat. I won't shake your hand because I'm not sure if I'm contagious or not. But my name is Brenda, and I'm very glad to meet you."

7

BRENDA

B renda's life was about to change.
　　　She was certain of it. All of her psychic senses were tingling and humming. It was as though this woman held a shard of Brenda's destiny.

The woman herself was beautiful. She stood in the doorway, slender and uncertain, black hair pulled off her face in a loose tail behind her head. Her nose was small, and her lips? Her lips were the shade of that old Victorian color sometimes called ashes of roses, the top lip fuller than the bottom. Brenda could well imagine what those lips would feel like, covering her own.

Brenda jerked her gaze away from the woman's mouth, to find the woman staring back at her.

Her deep brown eyes were sad. So very, very sad.

:She traveled far to reach you,: the Voice said.

"Please, sit down. Can I offer you any tea?"

"Tea would be great. Any kind is fine. Herbal or black. I'm sick of jasmine, though, so don't try me." The woman quirked her lips up in half a smile.

Brenda laughed. Then she noticed she didn't feel quite

so ill anymore. The slight tinge of nausea was still there, but some of the tension had fled her neck and shoulders.

"What brings you up to Portland?" she asked, as she filled the electric kettle and got out a teapot, cups, and a loose leaf Pu-erh tea. "I didn't think you made in-person visits."

She heard a sigh come from behind her, and felt the fear-tinged weariness roll off the woman and out into the room. When Brenda turned, the woman was clutching a gemstone pendant that hung on a silver chain around her neck.

Give her some privacy, Brenda, she thought, and turned to warm the pot, swirling hot water around it before dumping it back out into the small sink. She took her time measuring the tea into the mesh strainer that fit snugly in the blue ceramic pot, put everything onto a tray, and carried it to the table.

The ways of magic sometimes required charging in, working one's will in one decisive moment. But getting to that point required training. And training required patience.

Brenda had patience in spades.

Caroline still hadn't spoken. She clutched the gem, eyes open and staring at the quilted banner that represented Air on the east wall.

Setting the tea things out on the table, Brenda swept her tunic and skirts beneath her thighs and sat. She was used to sitting quietly. That was often the best way to draw people out, she'd found. Some needed questions; some needed a distraction; others, though? Just needed space and time.

She had a feeling Caroline didn't have anyone who allowed her to come to things at her own pace. At least, not for a long time.

When the tea had steeped long enough, she poured, and finally broke the silence.

"I'm sorry you've been hurt," she said.

Caroline just nodded, finally releasing the gem. It was an amethyst point, very high quality, in a simple silver setting. Brenda could see why she'd been clutching it. One of the qualities of amethyst was to help with emotional states.

"How did you know?"

Brenda smiled, and handed her a cup of the fragrant tea. "I *am* a professional psychic," she said gently. "But mostly? It's all over your face."

:*Tell her that if she stays with you, her life will feel safe again.*:

Brenda almost reeled with longing at the words. This voice, whatever it was, *whomever* it was, was either very wise, or a master manipulator.

Or both, she thought. It knew just what Brenda wanted, which really bugged her. No way was she telling this woman that she was the answer to her problems. As if. Brenda couldn't even keep herself safe these days. How was she going to protect this woman from whatever was dogging her heels?

Oh, Brenda could see that well enough. A shadow trailed behind this woman's aura, reaching for her like a malevolent fog.

Caroline sipped at her tea, delicate fingers wrapped around the teacup, brow furrowed.

"I'm sorry," she finally said. "My intention when I walked through the door wasn't to lay my burdens on you. I really did just think I'd waltz in, introduce myself, make an appointment to show you some stock, and go get an early dinner."

Caroline met Brenda's eyes then. "But it seems that

meeting you has thrown me off a little. Or maybe its just the exhaustion from the drive."

:Tell her.:

Brenda inhaled, willing air into her lungs, willing her muscles to relax again. *What has happened to you?*—she chastised herself—*you're supposed to be the mighty witch, the one people come to for help. And you're acting like a teenager or something.*

But there was no helping it. Whatever strangeness had surrounded Brenda these past few days seemed to be deepening. And the stronger it got, the more her confusion grew. For the first time in over a decade, Brenda felt well and truly out of her element.

:Tell her.:

She drank some tea, took a breath, and spoke. "This is likely going to sound strange. But I've been told..."

The air grew thick with expectation. Waiting. Caroline stared at her with those sad eyes, tea cup arrested in midair, eyes trained on Brenda's face.

"There's no way to say this that will make it sound any better. So...the message is that if you stay here, in Portland, your life will start to feel safe again."

Cheater, she thought. But Goddess knew there was no way she was going to announce that this woman was going to find safety with *her*. That was what every charlatan and cult leader told prospective followers.

Or that was what a romance-besotted, desperate person told the one they were desperate to hold on to.

It's also what abusers tell their victims, her own mind said. Right. And this woman had some of the hallmarks of that, didn't she? Brenda could see them now.

She risked sliding her hand across the table. Caroline, head down, saw the offer and slid her own hand across. She squeezed Brenda's fingers, just for a moment, before picking up her tea again and clearing her throat.

"Does this happen often?" the woman asked.

Brenda coughed and drank more tea.

"What do you mean?"

Brenda hadn't dated in four years, and hadn't felt this level of attraction to anyone in even longer. She really didn't want to blow it here. Not that she even knew who this woman was, or how long she was going to stay.

"People coming through your door, needing help. Do you give everyone a cup of tea, sit them down, and tell them the truth about themselves?"

"Only sometimes." Brenda smiled. "Only the ones that want to hear it."

Then why have you lied to her already?

Because she was afraid. Because, out of all the strangeness, the throwing up, the voices, the light...seeing Caroline walk through that curtain felt like the most significant thing of all. And it felt personal.

Too personal.

"You don't have to tell me anything you don't want to. No one owes a relative stranger their story. But I can also tell you that if you want to talk about it to anyone, I'm happy to be the person you tell it to."

"I have a confession to make...."

Brenda felt a flutter beneath her breastbone. Her moonstone pendant felt warm above her tunic.

"When I first came through the door, I thought you were an angel."

That shocked a laugh from Brenda's throat. "A *what*?" She practically shrieked the words.

"An angel. I'm serious. You still look like one to me. It

flickers in and out." She looked thoughtful. "Like an old film reel, or a double negative photograph."

"That's...very nice of you to say, since I happen to know I look sick as a dog."

Caroline frowned and shook her head. "Really? No. Oh, that's right, your co-worker said something about you being in quarantine. I forgot. But you *don't*. Not at all."

Brenda knew what she'd seen in the mirror that morning. A woman who had just heaved her guts into the toilet, and still looked touched by the Gods.

What in all the worlds is happening to me?

And what had brought this woman here?

"But to me?" Caroline shook her head again, rippling her dark hair over her shoulders. "You still look like an angel."

8

CAROLINE

C aroline stood on the porch of a pale linden-green foursquare farmhouse. The broad porch planks were painted brick red to match the door. The porch support beams were a lovely shade of creamy white.

She exhaled. The air in Portland was soft against her skin. It felt good here, as though maybe, just maybe, she could relax.

Pressing the brass doorbell, she waited.

An insistent, muffled buzzing came from her purse, snapping all of her tension back into place, hunching up her shoulders, and bringing back the queasy feeling in her stomach that had become too much a part of her life in the past few years.

Caroline had needed the GPS to find Sydney's home, but was regretting turning the phone back on already.

She ignored the buzzing. If it was a client, she could call them back. If it was Rafe? He could go to hell.

Or he could find you and kill you.

She shoved that thought down, deep into the depths of herself, and clutched at the amethyst tip resting on her breastbone. A shard of the good part of her life that Rafe hadn't managed to break.

"Caroline!" The four-panel door swung open, revealing a lanky white woman in faded jeans, with red wool socks on her feet. A shock of prematurely gray, short hair crowned her narrow face. Sydney's bright green eyes were framed by huge green-rimmed glasses and she wore a loose purple sweater over a white shirt. Always colorful, Sydney was.

Caroline had forgotten how much she missed her friend.

Sydney swept her into a huge hug. It felt like being surrounded by sunshine and warm flannel, and always had. Some of the tension receded.

"Where's your suitcase?"

Caroline pointed behind her on the broad porch, and Sydney grabbed the small roller bag and gestured her through the door.

So many doorways today. So many kinds of welcome...

"Wow. This place is amazing."

And it was. Polished, dark wood staircase. Polished wood floors. Eggshell-blue walls above dark wood wainscoting. Oil paintings. Carvings. Stained glass lampshades.

"Come on through."

Sydney led her through a wood framed doorway into a double parlor with burgundy walls and a box beam ceiling. A fireplace in the living room portion was flanked by two large windows, currently covered with royal blue drapes.

The second parlor was being used as a dining room. There was wood everywhere. Books. Art. Flowers. Rugs.

"Dan! Come on out and meet Caroline!"

Dan was huge. Taller than Sydney, with large shoulders encased by an untucked, unbuttoned, plaid flannel shirt over jeans. A white T-shirt showed that he also had a substantial belly. He was handsome and carried himself with ease. Brown hair trailed down to graze his collar, and a neat beard graced his pale brown face.

In his right hand was a wooden sauce spoon, with some sort of delicious-smelling tomato gravy around the rim. At his heels was a grinning yellow Labrador retriever.

"I'd shake your hand, but I'm in the middle of cooking. Hope you like chicken cacciatore, 'cuz that's what's on the menu."

"It smells delicious." She crouched down, dropping her purse from her shoulder and onto a dining room chair. "And who's this?"

"That's Bella, bella, dressed in yella."

"Hi Bella. You're a pretty girl." The dog walked toward her outstretched hand, toenails clicking on the wood floor, tongue lolling happily from her mouth. Her fur was soft as corn silk. Caroline felt the sudden urge to curl up on the floor with the dog.

"Well, welcome to our home, but I need to get back to cooking. Why don't you two come keep me company? Open a bottle of wine, lover?"

As soon as Dan walked back into the kitchen, Bella followed.

"Do you need to wash up or anything?"

"Just my hands. Should I put my suitcase somewhere?"

Sydney shook her head. "Leave it for now. We'll get you settled later. Come on through to the kitchen. You can wash your hands in the sink."

The kitchen was as beautiful as the rest of the house. Glass-front dark wood cabinets. A large island with a stove and chopping surface sat in the middle of the kitchen, with four padded stools at the counter portion opposite the stove.

"This house is truly amazing. How in the world did you afford it?"

Dan laughed. "That's all Sydney. She's the moneymaker of the family. I'm just the fix-it guy."

"He's modest. This place was a wreck when we bought it, which is part of why it was cheap. Dan's the one who turned it into a showcase. Plus, real estate up here is still half the cost of where you are."

"It's rising, though," Dan said, chopping bell peppers for salad. "A lot of people feeling the pinch right now."

"True enough. We're very fortunate," Sydney said, looking through a wine rack.

By the time Caroline had washed and dried her hands, there was a glass of pinot noir for her, sitting in front of a stool at the island counter. She took a sip, rolled it across her tongue, and sighed.

"Is that your phone?" Sydney asked.

Sure enough, a muffled buzzing carried through from the sitting room. Damn it.

"It's nothing," she said quickly. "I'll just let it go to voicemail."

"You sure about that?" Sydney raised an eyebrow. "Won't your husband be worried? I always text Dan when I'm away on business, to let him know when I've arrived somewhere."

Caroline didn't say anything. She just sat there at the counter, fingers wrapped around the bowl of her wineglass, jaw clenched.

Damn it. One night. That was all she'd been hoping for. One night to get her mind clear. Of Rafe. Of their marriage, and whether or not she actually had the courage to leave.

And if she did, what would her life become? Where would she live? What about her business?

And frankly, she even needed to clear her head about that woman, Brenda. Meeting her had been uncanny. One part of Caroline wanted to spend as much time with the woman as she could, and the other part of her felt way too exposed.

Plus, she found her really attractive. That kind of freaked Caroline out, too. Sure, she'd been attracted to women before, but only in passing. And she hadn't kissed a girl since high school. Not since Jenny Lynn.

Dan faced her across the kitchen island. "Is something wrong?" he asked.

Caroline raked her fingers through her hair, sweeping the rubber band off and undoing the heavy ponytail in the process. She shoved the hair band into the pocket of her jeans.

"What *isn't* wrong?" She took a deep drink from her glass, and blinked away a sudden rush of moisture in her eyes. "I'm sorry. My life's a mess and I think I'm only just now realizing it. I'm not sure how I got here, and have no freaking idea how to get out. Didn't mean to show up on your doorstep and fall apart."

"But that's why you came." Sydney place a hand on her shoulder. "I've known things were wrong for a long time, girl. And while I'm sorry it's taken you so long to figure it out, I'm glad you finally have."

"You have?"

Sydney nodded, and drank her wine. "You stopped calling me, Caroline. And the few times we did talk...you didn't exactly sound like yourself anymore."

Well, damn.

"What do I do?"

"You stay here, drink wine, eat this amazingly delicious dinner I've prepared, and tell us your story," Dan said.

The phone buzzed again. Just once. He'd left a message.

"So. What's going on with the phone?" Sydney asked.

"Rafe. He's been calling ever since I left Reno. Mostly, I've left the phone off."

"Reno? I thought you drove up from the gem show in Vegas."

Caroline looked into the purple-tinged liquid in her glass, as though something was going to reveal itself there.

"I was. But I told Rafe I had more meetings in Vegas. I was going to spend the night in Reno," she whispered. "But he tracked me there."

"What do you mean?" Dan's voice was quiet, hard.

She looked up. Looked from Sydney's green eyes behind those ridiculously bright green frames, and into Dan's golden brown, suddenly serious eyes.

"There was a tracker on my Jeep. He put it in the spare tire. I found it. Smashed it. Then I called you." She looked at Sydney, whose mouth wasn't smiling anymore. "I'm sorry. I shouldn't have brought this to your door."

"The hell you shouldn't have," Dan replied.

Sydney pulled her in for another hug. "You did the right thing, coming here. That husband of yours sounds like a controlling bastard. And if I find out he ever hit you, he's dead."

For some reason, that made Caroline feel a lot better.

"Thanks, you two. It means a lot. I mean, I've been a crappy friend all these years, and then just show up here..."

Dan poured more wine into all three glasses on the counter. "We have a huge home just for this reason. Well, that, and it's a kick-ass house. But you stay here as long as you want or need to. And if your husband comes around, I won't keep Sydney from ripping out his throat."

Caroline laughed. "That sounds good."

The phone started buzzing again. It hadn't even been thirty minutes since the last call. Sydney jumped up and brought the buzzing purse into the kitchen, holding it out to Caroline.

"Answer it, turn it off, or smash it into bits. Your choice. But it can't be buzzing here all night long. Dan hates anything that interrupts dinner."

Caroline pulled the phone off and powered it all the way down.

"That was my second choice," Sydney said. "But I guess it'll do for now. Dinner ready, lover?"

"Grab the plates."

Caroline exhaled, and threw the phone back in her bag.

Please, she thought, *let everything be okay. Please. Let everything be okay.*

Nothing felt okay.

9

BRENDA

Brenda was ensconced on the red sofa in Raquel's living room. Next to her own place, this was Brenda's favorite place to sit and relax. There wasn't a fire in the grate tonight, because the week had been so warm, but the space was homey and smelled good all the same.

Other coven members were scattered on the couch, and in Raquel's matching cozy arm chairs. Alejandro, the coven sigil and numbers guy, sat in a heavy rocking chair, dressed sharply as always.

Brenda liked Alejandro. She liked everyone in the coven, but Raquel was her best friend. They'd founded Arrow and Crescent together. She was a gorgeous Black woman with dreadlocks that flowed down her back, a warm voice, high cheekbones, and a ready smile. She was tucked up on the other side of the red couch, jeans-clad legs crossed beneath her, saying goodnight to her son.

Raquel knew Brenda more deeply than anyone, and loved her all the same.

"Give me a kiss, baby," Raquel said to Zion. "And don't

stay up too late reading or watching videos. Ten o'clock, okay?"

"Yeah, Momma. No problem."

Zion was a sweet kid, thirteen years old, smart, sensitive, and growing more handsome every day. He was already worlds apart from the young boy portrayed in the oil painting that hung above the fireplace. In the painting, he was around five years old, running, arms outstretched, mouth open in a laugh, with the orange and golden yellow rays of the sun behind him. A more fitting image of The Sun Tarot card, Brenda hadn't seen.

She had no doubt Zion was an empath who would need training any day now. Raquel wanted to wait a few more years, though she'd taught him some basics of shielding and some other energy management techniques. Brenda hoped she didn't wait too long on the other stuff. The kid was growing up fast. And growing into himself.

"'Night, Brenda. Tempest. Cassie. Alejandro. Selene."

"Good night, Zion," they chorused.

Brenda reached for a piece of cheddar cheese and a cracker. "Where's everyone else?"

"Lucy should be here already. Moss had one last-drop off, and I have no idea where Tobias is."

There was a knock on the front door, followed by the sound of thumping and rustling in the foyer.

A minute later, Tobias and Lucy both walked in, sans jackets and shoes.

"We brought more wine!" Lucy hoisted up a bottle of red. She wore her typical work shirt and jeans, and colored paint speckled her dark brown hair.

"Hooray!"

"You know where the glasses are," Raquel said. "And

bring in a couple of chairs from the kitchen if you want them, otherwise, there's the poofs."

Tobias ducked his head back into the living room, a wry grin in the center of his neat beard. "Did you just call me a poof?"

Raquel threw a cloth napkin in his general direction. It didn't go very far.

"If the description fits," she said.

Brenda was so happy to be here with her family. She felt a huge weight lift from her chest, as though maybe everything would be okay. More likely, though? This was the calm in the center of a rolling storm. A bright spring sky before more rain came.

You feel this good because you're avoiding what comes next.

That was the trouble with doing all this spiritual work: you ended up busting yourself sometimes. Brenda had trained hard to become honest with herself. It was the right thing. But it didn't mean she had to like it.

Brenda looked around at her friends. Activist Moss, who hadn't arrived yet, was the coven's conscience and Lucy, a Latinx house painter, backed him up by cutting through the bullshit every time.

Tobias, their resident white, gay hipster, was a talented herbalist, and redheaded Cassiel spoke with ghosts. Selene was as skilled in operative magic as anyone Brenda had ever met, even willing to do things like bindings and curses. Things that Brenda usually tried to avoid.

Each person in the coven had their skills, talents, and their role. Brenda hated that she was questioning her own role all of a sudden. But that was the other thing coven was good for. If you were feeling off, or avoiding something, you'd best bring it to the coven, and they would help to set you right again.

The newcomers made up little plates piled with olives, salami, and cheese. Cassiel handed around the bottle of wine, filling glasses. Brenda sighed. She wanted nothing more than to hang out for a while, and plan this month's ritual.

But that wasn't going to happen. She had to tell the coven what was going on with her. Arrow and Crescent was founded on honesty. The witch needed to be honest with herself, and honest with her coven, otherwise, the magic began to fall apart.

She'd already gotten "the look" from Raquel, and Tempest of course was already well aware that some "weird shit"—as she would call it—was going on.

Lucy and Tobias handed wineglasses to those who didn't have them, dragged out a couple of leather ottomans from the corners of the room, and folded themselves down in front of the food-laden, square coffee table.

"Shall we start with a quick check-in while we wait for Moss?" Selene asked, sweeping their long black hair back. Their face was always so pale, their lipstick perfect. Brenda knew it took effort for Selene to always look so good. They had to. It was part of their armor against a world that all too often didn't treat them very well.

The coven was gathered to plan their Spring Equinox ritual. Brenda knew what she had to tell them was going to take a lot longer than a quick check-in, but she was also aware that they couldn't go into a cross quarter ritual without knowing why she was so off balance.

Having one of the coven founders leading a ritual about the balance of day and night, winter and summer, when she was barely holding her shit together? Not so great.

She cleared her throat. "I need to go last, I'm afraid. I've got something going on that I need help with, and you all need to hear it."

Raquel nodded, and Tempest reached out and squeezed her foot.

"Well shit," Alejandro said. "I was hoping we had a break from..." He waved his hand in a circle.

"Yeah. I did, too, believe me," Brenda replied.

The front door opened, and Moss came in, shucking off his jacket to reveal a tattered Earth First T-shirt.

"Hey brother," Alejandro said, "come get some wine and cheese. Brenda has something to tell us."

Guess there wasn't going to be a quick round of check-ins after all.

What in Diana's name was she going to tell them?

"Tempest? Any clue where I should start?" she asked.

Tempest shook her head. "I could tell them about our customers coming in the shop this week, saying they hear voices, then bursting into tears, or running away. Or about you all of a sudden looking sick and pale, like you'd just been poisoned. Or about whatever it was that was going on yesterday with our gem distributor, and the new halo you have around your head, but..."

"Halo?" What the hell was she talking about?

"Come on, Brenda. I know you feel it. But, what I was going to say was, there's a bunch of stuff going on with you that I know you haven't talked about. So no, I don't know where you should begin."

Tempest sounded pissed off. Brenda didn't blame her. She must be worried. *I don't really have a halo, do I?*

"Oh, Goddess. I honestly don't know what to tell you all."

"Just try," Raquel said.

Her oldest friend in the Craft looked at her with a steady,

unflinching gaze. Her eyes were kind, but no way was Raquel letting her off the hook.

"I can tell you what I see," Cassiel said. "I see an angel behind you."

"That's impossible," Brenda said. *That woman, Caroline, said I looked like an angel...*

"Maybe so, but I don't think so." Cassie's voice was gentle.

Brenda set down her wineglass and put her face in her hands. She just needed the pressure on her forehead and her cheeks. Taking three deep breaths, she steadied herself.

"Eat some hummus," Moss said, holding out his plate, his brown eyes concerned.

Brenda's stomach lurched. "Oh no. I've been puking off and on for two days. I can't."

"So take another sip of wine and tell us...something." Raquel said. "Anything. You know we have a ritual to plan and you know we can't do that until we figure out what the hell is going on with you."

Raquel sounded sharp. Impatient. Brenda knew both things were true, but she also knew that without that, she wouldn't have the courage to say a word. Raquel knew her so well.

She took another drink of wine, took three deep breaths in, allowing her belly and chest to expand. Then she set her feet flat on the floor, sat up, and began.

"There's a voice. It isn't my intuition. It's not one of my Guides. It keeps telling me things about people. And people keep telling me things that *other* voices have been telling *them*. And it all feels connected. But I don't know how. People are in trouble. The voices are only part of it. There's...something." She shook her head, seeking the threads that felt just out of reach.

"I'm not sure yet. But it feels larger than just a new spirit guide, or the usual people coming to the metaphysical shop for help. It's...deeper. More troubling. And it's having a physical effect on me. Making me feel ill, but also strangely energized. Buzzing and humming with energy. It's weird."

Alejandro stared at her intently, sweeping his eyes around her body and her head. She knew what he was doing. He was trying to read her. In this sort of situation, coven members all had permission to read one another. It was part of how they kept one another in check, and made sure no one was going off the rails.

"Tempest is right," he said.

Brenda froze. *Nonononono.*

"I think there is some sort of angelic presence around you. It's actually trying to enter your auric field. No wonder you're having the symptoms you are."

Brenda shoved herself past Tempest and the others, and ran for the half bath under the stairs. Shoving the toilet seat up, she flung herself to her knees and heaved out a wash of red wine. She kept on until she was empty, stomach cramping, sour taste in her mouth.

"Brenda? Here. Let me help you." Raquel's hands were on her, helping her to sit back. There was the sound of water running and then Raquel was next to her again, wiping her face gently with a damp washcloth.

Brenda leaned into her friend's shoulder and began to cry.

"They're right. They're right. There was a shaft of light in my kitchen. I walked through it. It..."

"Shhh. It's okay. It what?"

Brenda took the washcloth and wiped her face again.

"It made me feel so afraid."

10

CAROLINE

The Road Home was truly magical. Walking through the door was like walking into the woods. The walls and ceiling of the shop were painted with a tall canopy of trees. Slender trunked birches with all-seeing eyes peering out from the white bark seemed to follow Caroline as she walked by, as though they were alive.

Caroline breathed in the scent of apple blossoms and cinnamon, a strange combination, but one that made her feel at ease. Taken all together, everything in the shop seemed designed to spark imagination. She would have loved a place like this as a teenager. It was just enough Tolkien fantasy mixed with the spice of real adult magic that it would've appealed to her younger self.

Caroline needed more magic in her life. That was why she started with the gems. Not only did the stones speak to her, she *wanted* them to speak to her. She wanted a life a little bit outside of the ordinary.

You're far from that now, aren't you? Instead of courting the extraordinary, you married a handsome man who wanted to keep you safe. But really all he wanted was someone to control.

Caroline shook off those thoughts. She was sick of them. Then she took in a deep breath, and coaxed a smile onto her face. Hand on her rolling case, she trundled into the shop. Frankly, smiling in a place like this wasn't hard. Fairy dolls flew among the display cases, dangling from the ceiling on clear filament. It looked as though they swooped and fluttered among the trees. When she turned the corner, she saw a small, red-capped gnome peering out from between two bookcases. One of the cases held books with illustrations of mythical creatures and mythical lands.

It was funny, she'd been supplying The Road Home for years, but had never really thought about what sort of shop it was. There were a lot of businesses like that; she just filled their orders and didn't give it much thought. When had she stopped wondering?

She was caught by a display of scented oils. The Rose Queen. Mystic Buttercup. Abandon Sorrow. Choose Love. Her right hand hovered between Abandon Sorrow and Protect Yourself. She probably needed both.

"May I help you with something?"

Caroline turned. The speaker was a mid-twenties white dandy wearing a crimson brocade vest, white shirt, black trousers, and crimson shoes. Perched on his dark hair at a jaunty angle was a top hat. Strands of dark hair curled out under the hat. They matched the mustache and goatee surrounding his ruby lips. What a character. Delightful.

Caroline let go of the rolling case and held out her hand. "I'm Caroline from Amethyst Gems. I took a detour after the Vegas gem show and wanted to stop by."

"Caroline! How wonderful!" He eyed her case. "I see you brought some stock. What a treat! Come back, come back."

He led her through a labyrinthine warren. How large

was this place, anyway? Some kind of remixed Renaissance music piped softly through the shop.

A long wooden counter curved around the back corner of the shop. There was a ruby velvet curtained door to the left.

"If you want to set some things out on the counter, I'd love to see them. It's a slow day today, and even if were disturbed, I can always take a break to help any random customers who wander in."

The shop was a prime piece of real estate. It was off the main street but that worked to its advantage, she imagined. It was on a corner, so while it looked as if you were walking into a dark warren at first, actually the back of the shop was quite bright. A bank of windows with stained glass strips at the top opened up onto a residential street.

"My name is Joshua, by the way. I figured you knew that but it also seems rude to not properly introduce myself." He doffed his top hat and gave quarter bow.

"Well, it's good to meet you, Joshua." Caroline couldn't help but smile now. The day was looking up.

As she bent to unpack the rolling case, she thought about the fact that ever since she arrived in Portland, she'd been shown nothing but kindness. How had she allowed herself to become so isolated? She barely even saw her parents anymore. Once they made it clear how much they disliked Rafe, it had just became easier to stay away.

You've lived ten miles from your parents all these years, she thought, *and you only see them what, four times a year? How did you let this happen, Caroline?*

"Do you want the good stuff first?"

"Yes please!" Joshua actually rubbed his hands together. Caroline laughed.

"You look like an excited child." She smiled up at him

and started lifting out soft velvet bags from the case and setting them on the wooden countertop.

"Feel free to take things out of the bags," she said. "I should've asked if you wanted to see gems first or jewelry. The ones I just handed you are set gems."

He drew a piece of large labradorite, chased and banded in silver, out of a bag and gasped, holding it up to the light coming in through the windows. Caroline paused to watch; she loved the way the peacock striations of the feldspar mineral caught and captured the light.

"That's a particularly nice piece, isn't it?"

They oohed and ahhed over gems and jewelry for the better part of an hour, Joshua pausing a couple of times to help some customers. Once Joshua had made his selections, she started packing up some of the things he wasn't interested in.

Caroline realized she hadn't felt this good in a long time.

Sydney had told her to take it one day at a time, and Caroline knew that was sound advice. That was really all she *could* do. There was no way to know what in the world was going to happen, what Rafe was going to do, or, she realized, even where she was going to end up.

So far, Portland seemed like a jewel itself. A place she could see herself making a home. But she also knew that that was getting ahead of herself.

And Brenda is here. The thought came, unbidden, as she rolled some stock up in Bubble Wrap, making certain it was secure. She shook her head at herself again. She had no time to think of love right now, not when it felt as if her life was going through a slow-motion implosion.

"Why don't you look around the shop before we settle up?" Joshua said. "It's always nice when my vendors can get a sense of who we are and what we do here."

"I need to stretch my legs anyway," Caroline said, and besides, she was pretty fascinated by this shop. She still couldn't put her finger on what kind of shop it was exactly. It was part fantasy bookstore, part metaphysical shop, and part pure whimsy. She strolled through the displays and books, pausing at a standing glass-and-wood display case filled with small icons, and pieces of silver and wood jewelry.

There were illuminated saints, halos picked out in gold leaf. There was St. George, slaying a dragon, and other figures, pointing upward or looking serene. Caroline didn't recognize most of them. She had been raised nominally Buddhist, but had had a couple of Catholic friends growing up, and now, running in New Age circles, she had definitely known some people into things like saints and angels.

Caroline? For her it had always just been about the stones.

A large silver oval caught her eye. The raised pattern in the center of the chunky medallion intrigued her. She wasn't certain, but it looks like a flaming sword crossing a large swan's wing.

"Did you see something you like?" She hadn't heard Joshua come up behind her, which was a little strange, but she wasn't paying as close attention to her surroundings these days, she guessed. Sydney's husband, Dan, would say that if she was going to remain safe, she had to change that. Well, she should work on that tomorrow.

Pointing to the medallion in the case, she asked "May I see that one?"

Joshua unlocked the case with the tiny key, and drew out the medallion, resting it inside her palm. "That's a powerful piece," he said. "It's tuned to the Archangel Michael."

"Are there stories about him? Or...I don't know, particular qualities he has? Like some of the rocks do?"

"He's a protector and a challenger. He often comes to people when they need him most." Joshua paused, looking uncomfortable. "I don't mean to intrude, and please tell me to mind my own business, but..."

"But you're wondering if I'm in some sort of trouble." Caroline sighed.

He nodded. A ray of yellow light from the stained glass shifted up and down on his cheek as he did so.

"I suppose I am. What tipped you off?"

"Well, I noticed you went for the Abandon Sorrow and Protect Yourself oils, out of the two dozen special blends made by yours truly. And then Michael? He's the big guns, you know."

Caroline didn't reply. She just stared at the pendant. It was truly beautiful. Modern. And she didn't want to let it go.

"In other words, you didn't come in here looking for gnomes and sprites." He walked back to the long wooden counter and unlocked a canted display case, drawing out a shimmering fall of silver. It was a heavy, close-linked chain. "This one suits the medal, and I bet it will rest just above that amethyst tip of yours. May I?" He held out his hand for the medallion, slid the chain through the loop, and said "Turn?"

Caroline did, lifting up her heavy dark hair. He clasped the chain and let go. As soon as she felt the chain and medallion settle themselves on her skin, she knew she needed them.

"There's a mirror over here."

Looking at her reflection, she saw that he was right. The sword and wing rested perfectly in the vee made by the longer chain holding the amethyst.

"How much?" she asked.

11

BRENDA

She tried calling Caroline, but the woman's phone went direct to voicemail.

It was funny: even in the middle of her own strangeness and upheaval, she couldn't get the woman out of her mind. Brenda wondered if she needed to do one of those "If your life was a dream, what would this mean?" exercises that she always assigned to beginning students.

If her life was a dream, and she started hearing voices, her customers started acting strangely, *and* a beautiful, lost-looking woman walked into her shop?

She would say...there were messages she'd been avoiding, that she needed to listen to. Avoidance was, of course, the likely reason for her pounding head and body aches. She knew that, too. But oh, how she didn't want to deal.

All right, Brenda. Take your own medicine. The coven had insisted she do more work at her altar, and call on her particular Goddess and God.

"*You aren't going to get anywhere with this by running away,*" Raquel had said.

"*We're here for you, Brenda.*" That had been Alejandro.

"And if you're meant to carry an angel, like Tempest and Cassiel think you are, we'll work with you on it. You aren't alone."

She didn't want to carry an angel, but they were right. She couldn't avoid this thing. Too many people were being drawn to the shop right now, needing help. If an angel showed up at the same time? It was all clearly connected.

So she bathed, slipped a loose purple caftan over her head, and settled herself in front of her altar. Not the bedroom altar, but the larger one that she often called her "working altar." It took up one wall of the spare bedroom she used as her home office. The altar had two tiers, the top one with images of the Gods and Goddesses she was most connected to: Diana and Lucifer.

That wasn't something she talked about much at the shop. People were still so frightened of that second name, thinking it meant "the Devil." But in the Gospel of Aradia, it was clear that Diana was the Moon and Lucifer, the Sun. The name simply meant "one who bears light."

He was often seen as a liberator.

If there were things you'd rather remained hidden, a being who bore light could feel very frightening indeed. Witches gained power by facing down their fears. It was time for Brenda to face hers. She needed all the illumination she could get these days.

These were not figurative statues—they were literal representations of sun and moon, made of brass and silver. She lit the votive candles in front of each statue, then recited a passage from the Gospel of Aradia.

"Diana was the first created before all creation; in her were all things; out of herself, the first darkness, she divided herself; into darkness and light she was divided. Lucifer, her brother and son, herself and her other half, was the light."

She bowed, then turned to the small side sections of

the altar, and poured out water from a pitcher into waiting cups. One cup was for the ancestors, the other for the descendants. A witch needed to know where she came from and honor where she—and the world—was headed.

Then she settled into meditation on the low cushion at the altar's base. Slowing her breathing down, she allowed her attention to drop into her core. She exhaled slowly, tuning in to the energy fields around her. Once again, all felt in order.

The disturbance wasn't there.

Which meant it had to be coming from outside.

Which didn't make her feel good at all. Her stomach and shoulder muscles tensed up again, and the aching started up at the base of her skull. Brenda sighed, and worked on relaxing.

Then she picked up her long, double-sided athamé and the birch wood wand she had gathered herself on the new moon, talking to the tree, leaving offerings, and then stripping, sanding, and oiling the wood. They were her most prized possessions, and for tonight's working? She needed to feel them in her hands.

Fire and air. Will and intention. Action and thought.

She was as ready as she was going to be tonight.

"Great powers of above and below, I call upon you. Powers of air, fire, water, and earth, I thank you. You who hold the sun and moon in your hands, I ask you, please, come to me now. Be with me. Help me to see the path I'm walking toward. Guide my mind and heart. Make quiet my fears. Strip away my ignorance. Allow me to continue to serve the great wheel of time, and those who come to me, seeking knowledge. Blessed be."

Then she waited. Breathed. She softened her gaze, eyes

flickering between the candle flames in front of the sun and moon statues.

And felt punched in the gut with fear.

Her body trembled and shook. She doubled over, in pain, then a force snapped her body upright again. Nonsense words—a strange series of guttural, repetitive syllables—poured from her throat. Hands shaking, she set the blade and wand down with a crash that rocked the altar.

The shaft of light appeared. Her vision flared and dimmed, over and over, as though the light strobed. But she knew it didn't. It was a steady, golden-white beam, the width of a person's shoulders.

:*Be not afraid*: the Voice said.

Brenda gasped, struggling to sit up straight on the cushion again. The shaft of light began to grow, until it was human-sized. She could still see the altar through it. It penetrated the altar and the space before the altar as though solidity held no restriction upon it.

Be not afraid? How was she supposed to manage that, when every molecule inside her wanted to run screaming?

She, who had faced her inner demons, who had stood in the presence of Gods, who had seen the worst life offered, and the best, how *was* she afraid? What was this thing that felt so foreign that it made her babble in strange tongues?

"Who are you?" she asked.

:*I am a messenger of the ever-living planes of existence. I am that which knows itself. I am that which bridges the spaces between formlessness and form. I am that which has one purpose.*:

Her breath came in small pants. She steadied her hands, and took in as much air as her lungs would manage, then held it in. Then she exhaled as much air out of her lungs as she could, and held that, too. Then she drew in another breath. She did this for four cycles of four. In. Hold. Out. Hold. In. Then she tilted her head back and breathed a stream of life-giving air upward, connecting to her higher self. She felt the column of her spine snap erect and into place. The rest of her bones and muscles followed suit.

Good. Her body at least felt calmer. And when the body could calm itself, so could the emotions and the mind.

She picked up her tools again, feeling the wand and blade in her hands. Brenda crossed them over her chest.

"Why are you here?" she asked.

:To remind you of whom you can become.:

That's cryptic, she thought. She also knew that was the way with a lot of these entities. They spoke in riddles, or stated things that were only obvious if you weren't occupying a human body here on earth.

"I don't understand," she said out loud.

The air in the room felt agitated, rippling like heat rising up from tarmac in the summer sun. Or the way the winds rose over the ocean come sunset. She wondered when the calm would come again.

"And the people who've been coming to see me this week?"

:They are but a symptom of something...:

It almost felt as though the presence was seeking out a word she would understand. Good.

:Something worse to come. Cataclysm. Apocalypse. You must seek out your strength to challenge and protect those who come to you in need.:

Fury filled her, driving out the final vestiges of fear.

"Oh, come *on!*" she blurted out. "Who the hell are you, and what are you doing breaching the wards of my workplace, home, and mind? How the hell did you get in here and who in the name of all the Gods and Goddesses sent you?"

:*I am the messenger of the ever-living planes of existence. Your anger is misplaced. I come not from this place your kind calls hell. I come simply from the great unfolding ways of space and time. My work is to carry messages to those who can bear the weight of them.*:

Brenda uncrossed her tools and raised her arms, holding the blade in her right hand and the wand in her left, pointed straight up toward the ceiling, and the sky beyond the roof of her home.

"Powers, hear me! My name is Brenda MacMillan, priestess and witch! I hold the powers of sight and sound. I see between the worlds and beyond. Protect my home, my business, my coven, and my friends."

Then she stared directly at the shaft of light.

"You are not welcome here, unknown creature, to sow fear and confusion in my life. Be you trickster, or deceiver, or the messenger you claim to be, I bid you to depart now from my home. Return only if and when you have clarity and true aid to offer me. In Diana's name, so mote it be!"

She swept the wand and blade out in an arc around her, making a cutting motion, circling the tools until they rested once again, crosswise, over her heart.

Slowly, very slowly, the shaft of light dispersed. She saw the altar clearly again. The votive candles in front of the sun and moon had burned all the way down and extinguished themselves.

"How?" *That wasn't possible*, she was about to say. But she knew it was. She had seen stranger things before.

Brenda sat for a moment, enjoying the fact that she could simply breathe. The tension was gone and her head felt clear.

She pressed her lips to blade and wand, and set them down on her altar once more.

Thanking the powers and the elemental forces, she closed the working, stood, and bowed.

"I need to eat something," she said to the empty room. It was true. For the first time since the Voice arrived, she actually felt hungry.

So, food first. The second thing she needed to do was to call Raquel.

12

CAROLINE

Sydney and Dan's kitchen was a sun-filled oasis. The famous Portland rains seemed to be taking a vacation while she was here, and while Caroline loved rain, she was happy to see the sun filtered through the big trees. It played through the kitchen windows set above the sink and counter area, next to the big, black, retro-style refrigerator, lighting up the white marble counters and the chili-pepper red of the kitchen walls.

The house was quiet, the hosts both at work. Bella the Labrador clicked her way into the kitchen to see what was going on.

"Hey girl, do you need to go outside?"

The dog just yawned, and flumped bonelessly onto the kitchen floor.

Caroline hoisted two heavy grocery bags onto the breakfast bar where she had sat the night before, drinking wine and eating chicken cacciatore. That seemed like an age ago. The terror and shaking fear was gone, replaced by a sense of goodness. Well-being.

Maybe it was Sydney's home, and the fact that she felt

safe here. Maybe it was meeting Brenda...which she wasn't still ready to think about yet. Thinking about Brenda made Caroline feel slightly giddy and ridiculous.

"You're only up here visiting, for one thing," she murmured to herself as she fished the gorgeous golden-yellow roses from one of the brown paper bags.

Or was she? Caroline had no idea yet. Her life was rapidly turning upside down. But, while she could imagine making a home up here, she realized that for the first time in her life, she couldn't imagine living in Silicon Valley anymore.

It wasn't home.

Everything down there felt constricted. Rushed. And thinking about going back made her teeth ache and left a sour taste on the edges of her tongue. It was the taste of the brown haze of smog from the traffic that increased more each year. The blue Bay Area skies were tinged with it now, especially during the warmer months.

Not Portland. Portland air smelled of pine, jasmine, and roses. She was sure the city had its problems—every place did—but maybe *she* wouldn't have so many problems here. Maybe she could become the person all her clients thought she was.

She ran her fingers over the new angel medallion. "What do you think, Michael? Do I have a chance up here?"

The medal felt good against her skin, as though she'd been wearing it for years. It hummed slightly, she swore it, as though it was forming a link with the amethyst crystal that hung upon her breastbone.

Caroline knew stones. She knew their properties—which ones were good for healing energy, and which were good for clarity of mind or grounding of spirit. She knew how they felt in her hands, she knew the effects that silver settings had upon them, but she'd never felt anything like this before. She'd never heard anyone talk about the way a stone might work when it met another power as great as its own.

That had to be what was happening. *Right?* she asked herself. If she'd learned one thing in all of her years around New Age types, it was that you should listen carefully, and then assess, whether it was a new situation, or a new gemstone.

And the sense she got from listening so far was that the medallion of Archangel Michael had called to her, and called to the stone she already wore. The shard of a once-mighty crystal cluster, shattered by her husband's anger.

Together, perhaps they would help her build a new life. Perhaps even in Portland, Oregon.

"Thank you," she whispered, touching the stone and medallion in turn. Then she set about unpacking the groceries she had stopped for on her way home. It was the least she could do; Sydney and Dan had been so gracious in taking her in. Caroline shook her head and smiled. She knew she was a mess right now. She was just grateful that Sydney didn't mind, and that her partner was a big bear of a protective man.

The kitchen really *did* already feel like home. She unpacked asparagus and early strawberries, a bag of spinach, and a packet of lamb from the butcher counter. She kept unpacking until the breakfast bar was filled with food. She inhaled the fragrance of the roses, admiring their startling shade of golden yellow. They were beautiful. She just needed to find a vase.

Grabbing a step stool, she began to hunt through the tallest cupboards; that was usually where people hid their vases, and other things that they didn't use very often. As soon as she opened the first cupboard, her phone buzzed on the countertop, vibrating its way across the tiles.

"Shit." She could hope it was Joshua from The Road Home, or another of her customers, checking on orders, but she didn't think so. The medallion grew warm, a small spot of heat beneath her collarbone. That was strange.

"Are you protecting me, Michael?"

She hoped he was. Lord knew she needed it. Caroline ignored the phone and scooched the step stool over. Climbing it again, she opened the cupboard and there on the top shelf, just as she had thought, were three vases. Two were crystal—one tall, one squat and round—but the third was a beautiful variegated clay tube made up of swirling shades of green, blue, and ocher. She had to stand on her toes to reach it, careful not to overbalance herself. The last thing Caroline needed was to fall.

The smooth vase in her hands, she shut the cupboard door, clambered back down, and set it on the counter. She glanced down at her phone.

Sure enough, it was Rafe's number. Missed call. She sighed. "Why don't you leave me alone?"

She was so sick of it. She actually felt astonished she had let it go on so long. How in the world had she let someone treat her that way? And why had she hidden it from other people? Her hands arranged the roses in the vase, careful of the thorns. The scent of them mingled with the ghost of coffee and bacon from the breakfast Dan had cooked that morning.

The phone buzzed and jangled again, and a thorn sliced into her thumb. "Dammit!" Shoving her thumb in her mouth, she almost knocked over the whole vase. She steadied it quickly, then glanced down at the phone.

Rafe.

"I'm done with you, you bastard; this ends now," she said to the empty kitchen. The refrigerator ticked in reply. She jabbed the talk button. "Rafe."

Immediately, he started screaming in her ear.

"I want you to leave me alone," she said.

His shouting was so loud, she set the phone down on the counter, and scrabbled in the pocket of her jeans for her earbuds. As she plugged them in, she felt almost as though she were floating. As if her body wasn't solid anymore. As if...she was watching and listening, half outside herself. Her emotions were muted. The room was still bright with sun, but slightly misty, as though someone had hung a pale, sheer curtain around her.

She felt her anger, that was definitely there. But she also felt calm. She slid the earbuds in, and heard Rafe's voice, still shouting at her. Thumbing the sound down, she felt... Michael. The warmth of the medallion and the humming of the amethyst crystal spread out and covered her, surrounding her.

It felt like being enclosed in a set of wings, and for the first time in years, Caroline felt as if she was going to be okay.

She reached her arms into the final grocery bag, only half listening to this man. Her husband. The one she thought she'd be with for the remainder of her life. Might as well get the groceries put away while they were at it.

"I'm done with it. I'm done with putting up with you. I've taken your shit for too long." *Good for you, girl, cursing at him like that.* Caroline heard him sputter. She opened the refrigerator and started shifting containers of leftovers, cartons of eggs, and bottles of juice aside. She needed to make room for the fresh stuff. "Yes, I'm putting away groceries while I'm talking to you. I already know what you're going to say, so it isn't as though I need to pay close attention. No, it's none of your business where I am."

That pissed him off. Caroline actually smiled. It felt good to feel so confident again. She hadn't felt this way since she was nine, at her first swim meet. She'd won first place that day. Sure, she hated Rafe's screaming, and the back of her mind still felt some fear, but mostly? She felt exactly as though an angel had her back.

13

BRENDA

Mount Tabor was beautiful. The tulip trees were in flower, the pines towered, children shrieked, and dogs ran and barked, happy to be outside when it wasn't wet and raining. The wind whipped pollen through the air. Brenda blinked her eyes against it, and sneezed.

Ah, the start of allergy season. Oh joy. All beauty had its price, and runny nose and eyes were a pain, but she was willing to pay it.

Raquel, her best friend of many years, her coven sister, her magical peer, or sometimes mentor and confidant, walked at her side. Raquel's son, Zion, scrambled up ahead, pausing occasionally to look at something on the ground. Then he would wave, and race ahead again.

It was cute. He was acting ten instead of thirteen. Spring had that effect on everyone, it seemed.

Brenda's quadriceps and the tendons around her knees began to burn. She'd been too sedentary over the winter. But it was spring now, and she felt it in her blood. Her body wanted movement, and outdoors, and lighter food. The attraction to Caroline was part of that, too. She smiled.

Despite Brenda's current problems, Caroline showing up in the shop was a good thing. It reminded Brenda that there was more to life than just work and coven. She was a woman with a sex drive. Maybe even a woman hoping to get laid.

Don't get ahead of yourself, Brenda thought. *That woman is clearly running from something. There's no telling what she needs.*

"So, you ready to talk some more about what's going on? About why you're so afraid of angels?" Raquel asked. She was barely out of breath despite the steep climb, damn her anyway. Brenda knew Raquel didn't have any more time for exercise than she did, but maybe running the café was enough of a workout on its own.

Brenda looked to her friend, the familiar face she loved so much. The dreadlocks tied back with a purple scarf. The full lips and high cheekbones. The dark eyes that saw way too much. Damn those eyes, she was going to have to spill, wasn't she? She couldn't keep anything from Raquel.

The fact that she'd asked for this walk today so she could talk to her friend didn't seem to make a dent in Brenda's avoidance. Gah. What was *wrong* with her?

"I don't suppose you'll let me wait till we get to the top of the hill?"

"Come on, Brenda, just rip the bandage off, why don't you? We already talked about some of it with the coven, and I know you didn't just ask Zion and me out for a walk today for nothing. Not that you don't like us, but..."

Brenda stared at the sunlight refracting into pinpricks and ribbons through the trees.

Raquel shook her head and started walking again. "I don't see Zion anymore and this mountain isn't going to walk itself. Let's keep going."

The two women leaned forward, arms pumping their way up the dormant cinder cone.

"Twice now, this shaft of light made me vomit. Does that sound like an angel to you? Really?"

Brenda rubbed the pollen out of her eyes and blew her nose with a tissue she found in her jacket pocket. Raquel took off her sweatshirt and tied it around her hips. The day was still cool, but walking up Mount Tabor made a person sweat in any weather.

"Yes. Actually, it does sound like an angel," Raquel replied. "Or some sort of powerful presence, at any rate. You want to know what else I think?"

No. Brenda didn't want to know.

"I'm so afraid, Raquel. I have been scared like this in years. I honestly..."

"You honestly don't want to admit you've been visited by an angel, and that it just may change the course of your life," Raquel finished her sentence. That's what psychic best friends do: they saw into your soul and finished speaking the words you didn't want to hear or say.

"I banished it."

"What you *mean*, you banished it?"

Brenda held up her hands, as if to ward off any opposition.

"Come on! It didn't announce itself. It just showed up in my life and started wreaking havoc. And how do I *know* what it is? What if it *isn't* an angel? I didn't banish it all the way. I just told it not to come back unless it was going to offer some actual help." Her breath was coming more rapidly and her steps slowed way down. Ugh. She really needed to get into better condition. "Besides, I'm a witch. I'm not some New Age flunky, preaching light and love and the Law of Attraction to cure all ills."

"Oh come on. I'm not buying all of that for one minute," Raquel snapped back. "Well, I'll take your point that we're not sure yet it whether or not the being is actually an angel. But the rest? Seriously? You are oh so not going to convince me that you're too good to work with angels just because you're a witch. You know as well as I do that the hype isn't the story. You know what angels actually are. Or you should."

Raquel gave her a powerful side-eye, then swept her arms around as if she could encompass every tree and bush on the bursting-with-springtime cinder cone. "Look around. If I were to tell you it's almost Equinox and I saw fairy behind that hawthorn tree over there, what would your response be?"

"Fine. Point taken." But fairies were fairies. Angels were...something else. Eunuchs. Tainted by too many years of white light.

Raquel kept walking. They skirted around an old chalet-looking building that must've been built in the '30s. Thank the Gods and Goddesses they were almost at the top.

"Point *better* be taken. If you can work with fairies and the Goddess Diana, and any number of your disembodied spirit guides, you can work with angels."

"I know." Brenda huffed. "Maybe I'm just having an identity crisis."

"Might that have anything to do with that woman you told me came into the shop?"

That startled a laugh out of Brenda. She practically barked with it. She knew just how the dogs felt.

"I don't think *that's* an identity crisis," Brenda said. "I do think that it may be some sort of spring fever. She's a little spooked, though. So I'm not even sure if anything is going to come of it."

They reached the narrow road that wound its way around the cinder cone. At the edge near the top, there was an old-fashioned brass water fountain. Brenda paused and swept her hair back from her face, then bent to taste the cool, clear water. Water from the Bull Run reservoir just north of the city. It was Brenda's favorite taste in the whole world and one of the things that tied her to this land.

Brenda stretched her legs a bit as Raquel took her turn to drink, looking across the grassy knoll at the top of the hill towards the big bronze statue of Harvey Scott, pioneer, newspaperman, and Republican. There should have been a statue of Chief Joseph up here instead, but that was the way of things. Rich white men got the statues, native people got worse than nothing.

"You hope something will come of it?"

Brenda nodded. "Yeah, I do, which is a nice thing to feel after all this time."

"And how are you going to figure out whether or not this is an angel or something else?"

"Well, I do have a shop full of books I can consult. And just today someone's been reminding me that I have friends that can help."

Raquel grinned at her. "I hear some of those friends are pretty good psychics. Maybe we could tune in, see what we can see."

"And if all else fails," Brenda said, "I guess I can always call on the OTO. They work a lot with angels and with demons, don't they?"

The Ordo Templi Orientis, a ceremonial magic group founded by the notorious Aleister Crowley.

"That they do," Raquel replied. "Shall we go see what Zion's up to?"

"Yeah, let's."

Brenda had to admit she still felt uneasy, but it was a beautiful day, and Raquel was right. She did have friends.

You need to stop being so stubborn, she thought. *You don't have to do everything alone.*

A man in jogging clothes ran up to Brenda, weaving and panting as he came. His face was pale, and he looked scared out of his wits.

"They won't leave me alone! Can you help me?" He stopped in front of the two witches, and clutched at Brenda's arm. She looked at his wild eyes, and felt a strange energy roiling around him, ripping through his aura.

Sowing discord, she thought.

She glanced over his shoulder, making sure Zion was safe. He romped happily on the grassy knoll, chasing a slobbering mastiff in circles, shrieking.

Raquel stepped forward. "Sir, let go of my friend, and then we'll see if we can help you." Her friend's firm tone snapped him awake, and he let go.

"Oh my God," he said. "I'm so sorry...I don't know what's happening. I'm so sorry."

"Why don't you sit down?" Raquel said, and gently led him to a bench next to the drinking fountain.

He sat, head in his hands, bent forward over his knees. His running shoes were fancy, neon yellow, and matched the stripes on his track pants.

Brenda sat next to him, as Raquel crouched at his side. She saw Raquel motion for Zion to stay away. That was wise.

"What's happening?" Brenda asked. "Are you in danger?"

He looked up, first at Brenda, then at Raquel. "Its... voices. It's as if they're chasing me. Telling me terrible, terrible things. Oh God, why am I even talking to you?"

"Because you know we might be able to help," Brenda replied.

"What are the voices saying?" Raquel asked.

"Different things. Sometimes they tell me I'm a failure, and that's why my wife left me. Sometimes they show me images of horrible things. People being beaten. Tortured. Raped. Other times?"

He was panting again, and bent back over his knees.

Brenda lightly touched his shoulder. "Other times?"

"They tell me to kill myself. And they make me want to."

Raquel looked at Brenda over the man's hunched form.

"This is bad," she said. "Is this what the other people are saying?"

Brenda nodded, feeling grim, as though all of the sunlight had left them, and a bank of dark clouds had moved in overhead. She looked up, past the towering stands of pine. The sky was still blue. "Some of them."

"I think we need to start gathering information. And I hate to say it, but that angel you just banished?"

"Yes?"

"You're going to have to call it back."

14

CAROLINE

Caroline looked around the bright, airy room. The big, plate glass windows of the restaurant let in every bit of the late afternoon sun, warming up the wooden floors and spilling across the mismatched tables, benches, and chairs. The place was called Savory, and if the smells emerging from the open kitchen hatch were any indication, the food here was pretty good. The place was vegetarian, which wasn't Caroline's first choice, but Brenda had suggested it.

She could see why. Besides being near Brenda's shop, the restaurant was bustling, and the open space somehow managed to feel homey despite the industrial beams overhead, crossing the high ceiling. Large black-and-white photographs of the city hung on the whitewashed brick walls.

"Excuse me." A muscular black man in a *Doctor Who* T-shirt startled her. "Are you in line?"

"Oh! No. Sorry, I'm just waiting for my friend."

The man smiled and scooted around her, joining the line to order at the counter in the middle of the room.

With a tinkling of jewelry, and the scent of jasmine wafting from her freshly washed hair, Brenda practically floated into the space.

Caroline couldn't help it, she felt warm inside just looking at the woman. Before she knew it, she was smiling, and Brenda was holding out her arms. Today's tunic was a delicate weave of blue-and-orange chevrons that draped enticingly over her slender frame. It was layered over black leggings and low-heeled black boots. The moonstone gleamed at her breastbone. It suited her. With her wavy dark hair piled up in an artful bun, stray locks cascading around her face, she looked beautiful.

Caroline walked toward her, and allowed herself to move into the other woman's embrace. She had to admit it felt good. Soft. Strong. Like a place she could hang out for a while. But she pulled back all the same.

After the two women separated, Brenda held onto Caroline's shoulders for a beat, blue eyes searching her face.

"I'm glad you called," Brenda said. "Are you hungry? I'm ravenous. Raquel and I went on a hike today. That's why I didn't answer when you called. And why I'm slightly late." She gestured to her outfit. "I figured sweaty and in hiking clothes wasn't a great way to show up for a date."

A date? Is that what Brenda thought this was?

Her face must have showed panic, because Brenda quickly squeezed her arm in reassurance. "Hey. I just meant...it doesn't have to be that kind of a date. I know you need to talk. And that's fine with me. Okay?"

Caroline nodded, and exhaled. *Chill out*, she told herself.

Then she realized that yes, she was hungry. She hadn't made herself any lunch after the conversation with Rafe. She had called Brenda right away and left a message. Then Caroline had sunk into the claw-foot tub in the bathroom next to her bedroom at Sydney and Dan's. By the time Brenda called her back and suggested they meet up for dinner, Caroline had forgotten all about lunch.

"What's good?"

Brenda perused the menu as they shuffled toward the counter. "I'm a fan of the yam noodles. And the salads. But pretty much everything here is good."

Caroline looked at the chalkboard above the counter and was relieved to find that they served beer and wine. After that phone call, she wanted a drink. And not a kale smoothie.

She could feel Brenda next to her, and Caroline found that her body wanted to lean towards her again. But she didn't trust that. She frankly didn't trust much of anything, except maybe the energy she'd felt humming between the medallion of Michael and the amethyst point. The necklaces were quiet now, but still felt good. Reassuring somehow.

They found a table for two tucked into a corner. The wood chairs were smooth, and the old table had been painted white at some point. Caroline sipped her pinot noir. It had a slight tang of vinegar. Not the world's most expensive wine, but it would do. It certainly wasn't as good as the wine at Sydney's house.

"So, do you want to talk about what happened?" Brenda's voice was gentle, pitched low to undercut the music and the conversations around them, just loud enough to reach Caroline's waiting ears.

The air felt thick all of a sudden, as if the atmosphere had increased somehow, sort of what it felt like walking into a sauna, but without the heat. Caroline's stomach lurched. She took another swallow of wine, and tried to steady herself with her free hand, palm flat on the surface of the table.

"Caroline! Are you all right?"

Caroline shook her head, trying to clear it, and looked at the woman sitting across the small table.

She gasped.

Light shimmered around Brenda's head. It looked like a halo, except more misty, less defined. Layers of purple shaded into a golden white, shifting color from her head outward.

"I don't know what's happening. I've never..."

The medallion at Caroline's breastbone heated up, humming and buzzing, talking to the amethyst. Talking to her heart? No. She didn't know.

"Just give me a moment."

Caroline sipped the wine, and let her eyes stray to Brenda's face, then to her lips. Despite the inner protestation that she wasn't going there, Caroline felt a strong urge to lean over the table and kiss the cranberry lipstick off of Brenda's mouth.

Maybe that was what the strange pressure change was all about. Now that she thought of it, it felt a lot like lust and attraction. That sense that your skin was reaching out toward the other person's. As if your molecules were thick, filling the space between your body and theirs.

She hadn't felt this in forever.

But that didn't explain the light still wreathing Brenda's head. Maybe she could just ignore all of it for now.

Caroline looked down into the wine glass, at the way the quirky chandelier overhead sending sparks of light into the ruby-colored liquid.

"My husband called," she finally said.

"Oh. Are you okay?" Brenda reached a hand across the

table. Caroline slid her fingers into Brenda's palm, and gave her hand a squeeze before letting go. She didn't want to let go.

Brenda continued, "I mean, I guess you're not okay or you wouldn't have called me. What I meant to say is, what can I do?"

Brenda's words made Caroline want to cry. She didn't know if it was just that she was still exhausted, or that it had been so long since she'd been able to unburden herself on others, and people just kept showing up to help. Sydney and Dan, and now this woman who was a stranger but was rapidly feeling like a friend. Tears pooled in her eyes. She pressed her fingers against them, trying to hold the water at bay.

"Shit," Caroline said.

Brenda handed her a clean tissue. Caroline wiped her eyes and blew her nose.

"Thanks. It's strange," she said. "I hate that he called, and I hate that he yelled at me. He's always yelling at me. But today?"

She looked at Brenda, and this time, she was the one who reached her hand across the table. Brenda's hands were warm around her own.

"Today?" Brenda asked.

"I felt calm. And I know this is going to sound strange, but I think it has to do with the medallion I bought from The Road Home."

"I love that shop! Joshua is a sweet, sweet man. Has a good business head, too."

Caroline took her hands back and reached for the medal, tilting it towards Brenda so the other woman could see the raised image on the silver, sword crossing wing.

Caroline swore Brenda blanched two shades paler than

usual. The cranberry lips and those blue, blue eyes stood out on the stark white face.

"Michael?" Brenda whispered, then looked into Caroline's eyes. "Is that the Archangel Michael?"

"It is." She wondered why Brenda was reacting that way. Almost as if she'd seen a ghost. That was a weird reaction for a woman who clearly had some sort of angelic presence around her.

A cheerful young Asian man with a shaved head and arms covered with tattoos set two heaping plates of delicious smelling food down on their table.

"Here's your curried vegetables over yam noodles, and the cashew and squash enchiladas."

"Thank you," Caroline said. "It smells wonderful."

"Bon appétit!" he said, and walked away, grabbing some empty dishes from the next table over.

Brenda was still staring at her, looking at the medal.

"Now it's my turn to ask if *you're* okay," Caroline said.

Brenda shook herself, then picked up her fork. "I'm fine. I just...there seem to be a lot of angels around lately. And something weird happened in the park."

They ate in silence for a moment.

"Angels are good, right?" Caroline finally said. "This one seemed to help me today. With talking to Rafe. Though I'm pretty pissed off he keeps calling. And you know, he put a tracker on my car. Did I tell you that?"

Brenda sipped her own drink, some fizzy, gingery concoction. She shook her dark hair.

"No. That's not good. It sounds like the behavior of a pretty controlling person." There was that gentle tone again. As if Brenda needed to tread carefully.

"You needn't be so diplomatic. Just because it took me all

these years to figure it out, doesn't mean that I don't see it now. Rafe is...not a very nice man. He's actually an asshole."

Brenda held her gaze.

"I feel lucky that I made it out alive."

"Let's keep you that way," Brenda said, raising her glass.

Caroline raised her own, clinking the wineglass against Brenda's glass.

"To life," Brenda said.

"To life," Caroline replied. "As a matter of fact, to a *good* life."

"Yes. Now let's figure out how we can help you establish that, shall we? We need to keep you safe and sound. And I think my coven might be able to help you with that. Alejandro is a whiz with electronics, and we have a lot of other talents in our group."

Caroline had to admit, she was relieved to hear it. She hadn't expected to come to Portland, Oregon. She hadn't expected to meet Brenda.

And she hadn't expected that a coven of witches and the medal of an archangel might just be the very things she needed.

"I'm really glad I met you," Caroline said.

Then she leaned across the table and brushed a kiss across Brenda's lips. Their fingers gripped each other, just for a moment.

Then they both sat back. Caroline smiled.

"Thank you for being here for me."

15

BRENDA

It was another Loreena McKennitt day.

The sun was still out, but clouds gathered once again, puffy white mixing with light gray, and more coming, just past the other side of Mount Hood.

Brenda bet there would be rain by the weekend. Strangely though, her head was better today, proving that her ailments were spiritual, not physical, despite manifesting in the body. Sometimes it worked one direction, sometimes the other. Each system influenced every other.

"Body, mind, and soul are one," she murmured, as her fingers separated out slim silver chains from silk cords.

She hoped the man from the park was okay. Neither she nor Raquel were exactly sure what to do with him, but Brenda had given him her card. Told him to call.

How can I help these people? She thought. Then she remembered Raquel telling her she needed to un-banish the angel. She dreaded it. Every cell in her body rejected the feel of it, the taste of it, and the unfamiliar Voice inside her head.

Why do you reject this? Brenda had to ask herself that question. Every witch did.

Her soul had no answers that day. All she knew was that she was worried. Worried about Caroline, about the people who kept crawling out of the woodwork, all hearing their own voices. Twisted voices. Voices that wished them ill.

She worked at the long glass counter, the only person working the shop today, though Tempest would be in soon. Brenda rolled her neck and shrugged her shoulders. Maybe she needed to book a massage with Tempest. The headache was better, but the tension in her body hadn't quite gone away.

Brenda realized she hadn't done even the most basic yoga practices in a week. That was always the way, wasn't it? The worse you felt, the less you wanted to do the very things that might help.

Once Tempest took over, maybe she'd take a walk. Get some air. Walking helped her think, and Brenda had time before the three readings she had scheduled for the afternoon. Speaking of clients, Brenda hoped she had the wherewithal to tune in properly, or if not, that the cards would carry her through. That was how it was at times. Some days the visions were so clear they practically crackled in the air. Other days were murky. Those were the days the witch relied upon her tools.

Brenda looked around, making sure the few customers were happy. No one seemed to need any help today, which was good. She needed a break from helping people.

She went back to sorting the jewelry shipment, getting some of the pieces ready for display. This was one of her favorite parts of the job, she had to admit. Brenda was part magpie, and loved her shiny objects.

Bells over the door chimed, and in walked the chief of

police, of all people. That was strange. In all her years of business, Brenda had never seen him cross the threshold. She went on high alert. It didn't seem like this was just a shopping expedition. If it had been, he wouldn't be in uniform, if he was caught dead in the Inner Eye at all.

Sure enough, he glanced around and headed straight for her. She set aside the jewelry she was sorting and waited. When he got close enough to the long glass counter, she spoke.

"Welcome. Chief Reynolds isn't it?"

She was shocked he would come into the shop. Some members of Arrow and Crescent weren't exactly favorites of the law. She wondered if he'd made the connection yet.

He took his hat off and tucked it underneath his arm. "That's right, ma'am. You Brenda MacMillan?"

He had a strange energy about him. Not just the usual combination of wariness, anger, and protection that so many police had about them. This energy was something... darker wasn't the right word. What was it? She softened her eyes and looked just around his shoulders and head. There it was, a swirling, red-tinged mist. It tasted of anger, sorrow, and some measure of fear.

It reminded her of the energy around the man on Mount Tabor.

The strange thing was, it didn't feel as though the mist was emanating from him. It was as though some other entity or thought form had entered his field, and made a home there. No wonder he looked so cranky.

"What can I do for you, Chief?"

"You're a psychic, huh?"

Brenda arched an eyebrow at that. She didn't mind answering people's questions, but she learned to tread carefully when they sounded belligerent or defensive. This man sounded like both.

Luckily, she was used to choosing her words. Clarity of speech was another of the witch's tools.

"Well, everyone has some psychic ability. I'm sure you have to use intuition all the time in your job, don't you? You couldn't function otherwise, and probably wouldn't have been promoted all the way to chief."

The man said nothing, but his mouth twisted, as though he'd just bitten down on something bitter. Some people didn't like hearing they were anything "woo-woo" or strange. Intuition was as common a talent as the power of speech, but people still liked to pretend it wasn't real.

"The only difference is that some of us train ourselves. It's just like any other skill; we can get better at it over time. I've been doing it for years, so yes, you could say that I'm a psychic." She smiled. "At least, that's part of what people pay me for."

He grunted at that, clearly unimpressed. Brenda wondered where in the world he was heading with this line of questioning. Out of all the strangeness of the week, including the Goddess-damned shaft of light or angel or whatever it was, this was edging up on the strangest.

He looked away from her, eyes not quite taking in the display of tarot cards, or the crystals, or the low cases filled with books across the room. "You know Tobias? He's a friend of yours, right?"

Oh no. Brenda didn't like the way this was heading at all. She turned and busied herself at the small altar set behind the counter. Picking up a lighter, she thumbed the wheel, until a flame *snicked* into life. She carefully set the flame against the edge of a charcoal round, holding it against the black disk until the edge began to glow. Then she placed it into the thurible, and dropped some amber chunks of frank-incense and myrrh onto the charcoal. They began to melt, sending a plume of sweet smoke into the air.

"I do know Tobias, he's a friend of mine. What did you need to know?" *He's also in my coven, as you know, but I'm not giving you any more information than I have to.*

This situation needed more than frankincense and myrrh.

Brenda could practically feel the red mist bunching and coiling around the chief. Whatever it was, it couldn't be good. For good measure, she reached down a jar of lavender and threw a few of the dried florets over the melting resins. The combination should serve to calm and clear the air.

"And he's what—dating?—that Aiden person from De Porres House?"

Right. Really not good. Aiden had been one of the main instigators in stopping the police sweeps of the houseless camps in February. The chief and the mayor had not been pleased. The sweeps had stopped, anyway, and some reforms were said to be on their way.

People didn't like it when you shifted the balance of power and they were one of the power holders. Aiden had certainly worked hard to shift the way things were going in Portland, and Tobias and the coven had been part of that. The chief of police didn't need to know just how much a part.

"You curse people?"

Well, that came out of nowhere! Brenda coughed.

"Excuse me?"

He waved a hand around. "You know. Curses. Bad juju."

Brenda glanced through the shop, making sure her customers still seemed content and that no one was close enough to overhear the bizarre turn the conversation had taken.

"I truly have no idea what you are talking about, Chief. I'm not in the habit of cursing people." Though sometimes, yes, she and the coven gave people who needed it an energetic shove. But there was no way she was getting into the finer points of magical operations with the Chief of Portland Police. Not when he was questioning her.

"So you're not actively working against the PPD?"

That stopped her in her tracks. She heard the pang of fear in his voice. Something was wrong. She made sure her voice was pitched low, so it wouldn't carry.

"Why do you think I'm working against the police department? What exactly is going on?"

He looked around this time. Two of the customers waved and walked out the door, leaving only one person in the shop. The woman was now ensconced in one of the two comfortable reading chairs in the book area. She seemed engrossed and unlikely to eavesdrop.

"Chief?"

He wiped one of his large, wind- and sun-reddened hands across his mouth.

"I've been..." He shook his head, and put his cap on the counter, then leaned in close, dropping his voice so low that Brenda had to lean in, too. She smelled cinnamon on his breath, and dried sweat.

"I've been hearing voices. I swear it's like someone is standing next to me, talking in my ear."

Oh no. *Here we go.*

"You aren't the only one. There...seems to be a lot of that going around lately."

He wiped his face again. "And you got nothing to do with it?"

"I swear. Whatever is happening right now? It isn't coming from me, or my coven, or anyone else I know."

But she was starting to suspect she did know the source. Damn it. She was so going to give Raquel an earful about this. The coven, too. *"Just accept that it's an angel, Brenda. Don't be suspicious."*

Yeah, well. Brenda might look like a middle-aged light-worker, but she was still a witch, dedicated to the huntress, Diana. Priestess of the moon.

The chief looked a little disappointed. He'd really wanted her to be the culprit, and the answer to his problems.

"Well, all right then. But I'm not going far. And if I do hear you're doing any..." He waved his right hand in a circle.

"Any what, Chief Reynolds?"

"You know." He put his hat back on his head. "Have a good day, ma'am."

"Chief Reynolds!"

He turned back.

She lowered her voice again. "What are the voices saying?"

He grimaced. "They're talking about being raped."

Then he turned and walked back out the door, bells clanging behind him.

And left Brenda, still standing behind the shop counter, wreathed with incense, wondering what in Diana's name she was going to do.

Call back the damn shaft of light?

The thought still made her feel sick.

But she knew that sometimes that just meant she was on top of a task so big it terrified her.

And that terror often meant it was just the thing she needed to do.

16

CAROLINE

C aroline was still getting her bearings in the new city, and had decided to walk the neighborhood near the little shopping area that held the Inner Eye and The Road Home. The trees were spectacular. Maples. Ginkgos. Tulip trees.

She supposed she would need to branch out if she decided to stay. She'd need to see what else the city had to offer. But for now, it was pleasant to walk around this beautiful neighborhood, admiring the houses, imagining herself living in one of them someday.

Maybe. She still had no idea how all of this was going to work out. It was pretty clear she would need to deal with Rafe soon, and get divorce proceedings started. If she didn't jump on it, she knew, he would make certain she ended up with nothing.

Any way that man could punish her, he would.

Caroline wrapped her jacket around herself, doing up the snaps down the front. She had just bought the quilted blue jacket, along with a green silk scarf, from a shop off of Hawthorne street. The coat stopped halfway to her knees, and brushed at her jeans as she walked, making a friendly swishing sound.

Caroline liked the warm comfort of it, and had been assured that it was water resistant. She'd been advised by the woman who sold it to her that she'd need an outer shell to get through sustained downpours, but Caroline figured she'd see whether or not she was going to stay.

She'd take her jacket purchases one step at a time, the way she was taking this whole journey she'd been plunged into. Purse slung across her body, hands tucked into the jacket pockets, she inhaled the scent of jasmine and laurel, and the hint of coming rain.

Her stomach growled. Wondering if Brenda was free for lunch, she headed back toward Hawthorne, figuring she'd stop into Inner Eye, just in case.

"Hey! Caroline!" She recognized the voice and began walking faster. How in the hell had he found her? She'd said nothing to Rafe about her location, just that she was spending some time with an old friend while she thought things over. At least, she'd tried to say all of that, in between his shouting.

"My phone. He must have traced my phone somehow." She should've thrown it in the garbage when she smashed the tracker. "Dammit."

She kept her head down, steering her boots towards Hawthorne. It was only two more blocks and then she'd be safe. Surrounded by people.

Car door slamming. Feet rushing up behind her. Caroline ran.

Oof. Body slammed into brick. The wind knocked from her lungs. Arms wrapped around her. Clutching. Grabbing. She whipped her body side to side, struggling, fighting.

"Rafe! Let go of me!" She kicked and scratched and heard him curse.

"I just want to *talk*." One arm wrapped around her torso she clawed and bit, and then, pressure against her windpipe. He held his arm in a bar across her throat and began dragging her backward.

Carolyn wished she had screamed when she had the chance. Now it was all she could do to fight for air. He dragged her out into the street. She flailed, still kicking, her boots scraping on the tarmac.

Then he was shoving her in his car. Locking the door. Smell of leather and sour sweat.

She saw spots, and shook her head to clear it. Breath heaving in and out of her chest, she reached scrabbled at the door handle, just as he swung into the car, and shoved her backwards, slamming her head against the glass.

The locks clicked.

She could've sworn she heard her name in the thirty seconds his door was open. A woman's voice. Brenda?

Rafe put the car into drive, did a three-point turn, and raced off down the street.

She scrabbled at her door again and Rafe slammed on the brakes, flinging her forward. Caroline's head snapped forward, then back. Shit. She didn't want to seatbelt herself in, but he was going to make her pay if she didn't. Horns blared behind them.

"Shut up," Rafe muttered, then clicked a handcuff on her left hand, securing the other cuff to a special I-bolt attached to the cup holder.

"You *planned* to kidnap me? Bastard." The cuff was tight, digging into her wrist.

He said nothing, just reached across and pulled her seatbelt across her chest before snapping it into place. He put his own on, then put the car in gear and raced forward to the next light. It turned amber and then red as they sailed through. More honking. Tires screeched. Rafe didn't seem to care.

"What are you doing, Rafe?"

His mouth was a grim slit, his knuckles white on the black steering wheel of his Lexus. The car was his pride and joy. He took it to the car wash weekly and got full detailing. She looked down at the bolt securing the cuffs. She couldn't believe he done that. Had marred the interior of his precious car.

Had prepared in advance, making sure she couldn't get away. This was so not good.

"I have people waiting for me, you know?"

"You a lesbian now? Is that why you left me? Is that who's waiting for you?" He careened down the street, dodging cars and pedestrians, blowing through a stop sign.

"You're going too fast! And I don't know what you're talking about."

He made a sharp left turn, and she jerked against the seatbelt hard enough to bruise.

"That woman. The hippie chick in the floaty clothes. I've seen you with her."

Caroline started to shake, suddenly ice-cold despite the heat blasting in the car. How long had he been watching her? Following her?

"What are you talking about?"

His hand cracked across her face. "That woman!"

Caroline cupped her cheek with her free right hand. She felt blood on her fingers. His signet ring had cut her. Stanford. Another thing Rafe was so proud of. Who the hell cared what university you'd gone to once you passed thirty? Rafe did. Any social proof he could grab onto, he'd take it.

"She's a client. She buys product from me!"

He grunted, then turned his head and spat at her, just missing her face. A glob of white dripped down her new blue coat.

As bad as things sometimes were with Rafe, she'd never seen him like this before.

"So," she ventured. "You said you just wanted to talk. We're here, now. Let's talk."

"Too late. You shouldn't have run."

She took in a slow breath, trying to stop her shaking. Caroline needed to keep her voice calm. She unsnapped the top of her coat, trying to get some air.

"I was scared. I didn't know who it was."

"You knew."

He was right. She did know.

"I didn't expect you."

They were heading toward the river, the one that ran from north to south. She didn't remember which one this was. Was it the Columbia? The Willamette?

Not important, Caroline. Her brain was scrambling now, grasping for anything that might make sense.

Shops made way to industrial warehouses and railroad tracks. Rafe pulled the Lexus into a mostly deserted parking area. A train rumbled by, whistle blaring, wheels screeching and huffing on the tracks. Bells clanged and red warning lights flashed.

He turned the car off, and sat staring at the train. Car after car after car of flaking metal shipping containers rolled by. Caroline waited, taking an inventory of her injuries. A wrenched shoulder. A bruised neck. The cut on her cheek. She felt that swelling already. And she must have twisted an ankle.

Finally, the train passed. The warning bells ceased

clanging, and the red-and-black striped bar arms raised themselves again.

He stared out the window. Caroline didn't know if he was looking at the gleaming river, or at some scene inside his head.

Finally, he inhaled, about to speak. "You shouldn't have left. And you shouldn't have lied to me."

"I..."

He held up a hand, threatening to strike. She fell silent.

"You shouldn't have lied to me," he said again. "If you wanted to visit your Portland friend, or your 'clients'..."—he made air quotes around the word—"you should have just told me."

You never let me visit any stores except the ones directly en route to the big gem shows, she thought.

"Right?" he said, whipping his face toward hers. His eyes were dark, almost all pupil. Was he *on* something?

"I thought you wouldn't let me," she whispered.

"What? What did you say? I didn't hear you."

Caroline fought to control her shaking. Fought to not shy away. To remain calm.

She cleared her throat.

"I thought you wouldn't let me."

Her right hand slid through the vee at the opened top of the coat, underneath the green silk scarf, and curled around the medal of the Archangel Michael.

Help me, please.

"What are you doing?" Rafe's voice was as sharp as the beveled edge of his ring. Caroline could feel the tension coiling in him, ready to lash out again.

Shit.

"Nothing. Just loosening my scarf. I'm hot." She dropped her free hand onto her lap.

17

BRENDA

B renda breathed in the late morning air as she walked back to the Inner Eye. She felt grateful to be alive, and to have had short break from the shop.

The angel or whatever it was had been quiet for the past twenty-four hours, and, though she was worried about what the police chief had just told her, Brenda was determined to not get knocked off from her center today.

She wondered what the Equinox would bring. She prayed for balance as she walked. *May light and dark, day and night, teach us what it means to softly tilt with the cosmos, balancing strength and weakness, fear and hope, love, joy, and power.*

The coven's traditional Equinox Prayer ran through her mind, keeping time with her light boots as she turned the corner that would take her to the shop.

Four blocks up was a woman who looked a lot like Caroline. A dark-haired man had his arms wrapped around her, and looked like he was forcing the woman into a fancy car.

Brenda ran toward the car, shouting, "Caroline!"

The man turned toward her, scowling, then climbed into the car.

The car sat there. Good. Maybe she had a chance to get to Caroline before they took off. She was certain it was her, despite the distance.

She raced toward the car—she could see now that it was a dark blue Lexus—purse flapping and banging. Right. Her purse! She fumbled for the phone tucked into the bag's front pocket.

She paused for a moment to key it open and click on the camera. Running closer, her eyes darted between the back of Caroline's dark head and the license plate. Not close enough yet.

Brenda ran, full out now, purse still bashing against her hip, boots clattering on the sidewalk.

"Excuse me!" She rushed past a man securing a toddler into a massive jogging stroller that took up most of the sidewalk. Brenda ran out into the street. The Lexus revved, ready to go. She snapped three photos, as quickly as she could, just hoping one of them came out.

The car did a three-point turn and raced back toward her. She leapt out of the street, stumbling into a parked Toyota, and saw the woman's face as it flashed by.

It was Caroline. She looked terrified.

"No! Caroline!"

Brenda raised her right hand and began to pray out loud.

"Goddess Diana, send your hounds to follow and find Caroline, my friend. Lucifer, shine the light of the sun upon her. Give her courage and strength."

She gave a small push of energy out of her hand, and sent the prayer winging after the receding taillights of the car.

"You okay, lady?" It was the man with the stroller. He looked concerned. "Do you need me to call someone?"

"Did you see what happened?"

He stopped and waited as she stepped back up onto the curb between two cars, and pushed her way between two rhododendrons.

"What happened?" he said. "I was getting Carlos here all strapped in, so I wasn't paying attention. I just heard you shouting and then that car raced by."

Damn. She could have used corroboration.

"Never mind. I think my friend was just forced into the car, but can't be sure. I was hoping someone besides me had seen something."

She looked up and down the street. No one. Everyone was at work, she supposed. Or indoors eating lunch.

"Sorry," the man said. "If there's anything I can do to help, I'm happy to give you my number, but really, I didn't see anything."

Brenda nodded. "That's okay. I'll figure it out. Thanks."

She stood a moment, feeling the ache in her hip where she'd hit the car. And her boots were scuffed now. She hoped they weren't ruined.

As if that matters, Brenda. Right. There were more important things to think about, like what in Goddess's name she was going to do? Calling the coven was on the list, that was for sure. Should she call the police? She had no proof of abduction....

:Alejandro knows how to help you.:

It was the Voice again. It was back, damn it. But at least this time, it seemed like it was offering some useful information.

She hurried to the shop. The coven needed to be notified, and maybe Caroline's friend, Sydney.

:*Joshua.*:

Joshua? Why would...?

The archangel medallion. Michael. Right. If he sold that to Caroline, he might have some insight into what was going on.

Any port in a storm, she thought, then sent up another quick prayer. "Michael, if you hold the powers people say you do, protect Caroline with all your might."

She was at Hawthorne right now. The bustling street, which usually filled her with such joy, barely registered today. All she saw was a series of obstacles between her and the Inner Eye. Weaving in and out between pedestrians, dogs, baby strollers, toddlers tugging at their parent's hands, and houseless people selling newspapers, Brenda remained intent on her task.

"Hold tight, Caroline. Stay strong," she murmured. The man had to be Caroline's husband. But how in the world had he found her? What was he doing in Portland?

:*Alejandro.*:

"Okay. Okay. I'm almost at the shop. Just give me a second."

Her priestess self had taken over the panicked woman who saw someone she cared about abducted. Despite wanting to stand in the middle of the sidewalk and scream and cry into her phone, Brenda wasn't going to do that.

A priestess and witch acted from strength and centered-ness. The Inner Eye was going to help with that. She needed the clarity and protection of all the years' worth of wards, the prayers of peace and contemplation, and the scent of magic itself.

Brenda trusted that her prayers had landed, and what protections she'd been able to send to Caroline were in place. But their connection wasn't strong yet, so she didn't know how long they would hold. She needed counsel. Input. Help. She needed the threads of magic she didn't hold herself, but that others in Arrow and Crescent did.

She also needed a war room, and the back room of the shop would serve quite well for that.

"Rafe, if that was you dragging Caroline away, you have no idea what's about to hit you."

18

CAROLINE

Michael, *if you can hear me, and if you're a protector like they say...please. Help me now.*

Caroline couldn't stop shaking. The medallion had felt good for the three seconds she'd been allowed to hold it. If only...

:Don't move.:

Who said that? Michael?

Her eyes darted around the car. From the river outside, to the train tracks, to the glob of spit, slowly drying on her jacket. Anywhere but at Rafe's face.

She tried a deep breath and almost choked. Rafe must be on something. A stinking, chemical sweat smell crossed with the spice of his cologne. It made her want to vomit.

Keep it together, Caroline. But she couldn't. Not with a handcuff on her wrist and no way to call for help without him taking her phone from her. She backed as far into the space between her bucket seat and the door as possible without scraping the skin from her left hand. She angled her body toward Rafe, keeping her eyes on her lap.

And on the handcuffs.

When she cheated a look up, she saw him staring past her, out the window. Was that good or bad?

Must be good. He wasn't focused on her for now.

Don't piss him off. Don't piss him off. Don't piss him off.

The phrase synched with her heartbeat, so familiar. It had been her refrain for years. The only time she was free of it was at the gem shows, surrounded by raw rubies, tourmaline, and quartz. Talking with like-minded people.

Feeling as if, for once in her life, things were filled with beauty. With light. And that she was normal. Respected, even.

Don't piss him off. Don't piss him off. Don't piss him off.

Caroline was suddenly quite weary of the voice. *Shut up.*

She raised her face, just enough to look at him, but not enough to signal a challenge. That was a thing wolves knew. Or dogs.

"Why did you shove me in your car? And why am I handcuffed?" She spoke clearly, softly, carefully.

His pupils were so black, like onyx stones eclipsing the sun.

"Because you're a bitch. And you disobeyed me." His voice was cold. Cold was more dangerous than hot. Hot was scary and random, but cold always meant that Rafe had a plan. Caroline had learned to avoid cold at all costs.

Too late.

Michael, help me. I need to be strong.

Strength would either save her, or get her killed. But, frightened as she was, she knew somehow that this moment was the one in which she had to make her stand. To draw her line. To say "enough."

She just wasn't sure how yet.

There was a pattering on the glass. The rain had come.

"Why did you leave me?" He held her gaze with those scary, onyx eyes. He swallowed. "You know you shouldn't have done that? Don't you?"

One hand snaked out and softly stroked her cheek, then pinched, hard, right over where his ring had cut her.

She grit her teeth, fighting not to hiss in pain. Her eyes snapped shut for an instant.

"Look at me," he commanded.

She did.

"Why did you leave me?"

This was it. There was no way to placate him. No way to keep herself safe anymore. She was trapped in this car on the edge of an unfamiliar city, handcuffed and helpless.

She might as well be honest. He was going to punish her anyway.

"I haven't been happy. Not for a long time, Rafe."

"Why?" He frowned, brow furrowing, as though he were truly confused.

"You're angry a lot. Sometimes you scare me."

"Oh, baby, I just do that to let you know when you've done something wrong. I thought that was our arrangement. Wasn't it? That I would correct you when you're wrong?"

"No," she whispered.

He leaned in, close. Too close. The acrid, chemical sweat stink of him filled her nose and throat, choking her. She fought not to gag. She used to love the scent of Rafe's cologne. That was a long time ago.

He cupped the back of her head, bumping his forehead up against hers.

"It was, though, Caroline. It *was* our agreement." His

fingers dug into the back of her skull, right where it met her neck. His hand fisted into her hair and he yanked.

She did hiss that time. He pulled, tilting her head backward, then jerked her skull against the glass.

"Do you want me to undo your handcuffs?"

She worked to swallow. The angle of her neck was all wrong.

"Yes," she finally gasped out.

"What do you say?"

"Please?"

His lips were almost on top of hers, his breath warm on her lips and cheek. He smelled sour, like desiccated leaves and vinegar mixed with whatever chemicals coursed through his bloodstream.

"Please what?"

"Please, lover. Would you please take my handcuffs off?"

He released her head so quickly it slammed against the window again. She tasted bile and swallowed it down. Lover. She had started calling him that when they were still young. Before he changed.

Rafe insisted she continue to use the word. Insisted that she didn't love him if she didn't. Then the accusations began. The questioning. Did she have another lover? Was that why she didn't use that word anymore?

And so she used it. Every time.

Don't piss him off. But that wasn't as important right now as the fact that if he took the handcuffs off of her, she had a fighting chance. *Be smart.*

Calling him "lover" meant she was knuckling under. Kneeling to his authority. Giving him what he wanted.

With a jangle and a click, the handcuff was off her wrist. She rubbed the chafed skin, cradling her wrist up against her chest.

Up against the amethyst tip. And Michael.

She slid a finger and thumb around the medallion, feeling the raised bumps of the wing and the archangel's sword.

Help me.

"What do you keep touching there?"

With a rough thrust of his right hand, Rafe shoved the green silk aside, fingers closing over her own. He tugged. Caroline felt the chain digging into the soft flesh on the back of her neck.

Help me. Archangel Michael. Help me. Help me now. I beg of you. I plead with you.... The words tumbled through her mind, faster and faster.

The medallion grew warm against her skin and began to softly hum. It connected to the amethyst tip with a sharp zing that caused her to gasp.

"What is it?" Rafe slowly pried her fingers from around the medal, tugging on the medal and the chain. Caroline tried to get her fingers between the chain and her neck, to ease up on the tension as the chain cut into her skin.

"Just a necklace. You know I like necklaces."

"You know I like necklaces, what?"

"L-lover." God, that made her feel ill. Sick spit filled her mouth again. She swallowed it.

"What is it? An angel? Since when... Holy fuck!" He dropped the medal and shook his fingers off in the air. Then smacked her face, slicing through the skin over her cheekbone with his ring again.

Grabbing the medallion, he pulled. Hard. She wrapped both of her hands around his and pulled back, leaning against the seat back with all of her might.

Rafe bellowed and sucked in air between his teeth. "Let go of me! It's burning me! Motherfucker!"

Michael, help me. Michael help me. Michael help me.

The scent of burning skin filled her nose. Rafe's screaming filled the car.

Caroline held on.

19

BRENDA

The coven was gathered in the back room of the Inner Eye, sitting in a circle at the big table under the Elemental banners that hung on the four walls. A few people drank coffee from to-go cups. Brenda hadn't made any tea. She was too agitated, and couldn't stop pacing. She wanted to be *doing* something instead of planning, and it was making her crazy.

But she knew planning was necessary. She just wished it would happen faster.

Not everyone could make the meeting, and Brenda was frantic with it, even though she understood.

Raquel and Cassiel had to keep the café open, and Lucy was in the middle of a big job refurbishing an old Victorian, but Alejandro, Moss, Selene, and Tobias had all been able to rearrange their clients and schedules and make it.

She felt Raquel's absence the most.

Tempest was in charge of the shop, and had called to reschedule all of Brenda's clients. No way was she giving readings this afternoon. She was too scattered, for one thing. And finding Caroline took priority.

Alejandro was hard at work, tapping at his laptop. It had been his idea to track Caroline through her phone.

"If her husband was able to trace her that way," he'd said grimly, "we may be too."

"Is that even legal?" Moss asked, chewing on some sunflower seeds.

Alejandro just looked at him. "What do you think?"

Alejandro had explained that Rafe had likely used some sort of family tracking app, accessed through their phone plan. It was the sort of thing parents used to keep an eye on their children's whereabouts.

But tracking someone's phone outside of that sort of system was going to be tricky.

Alejandro was starting to sweat. Usually he was so perfect, but Brenda could see the sheen of perspiration on his face and darkening the pits of his pale purple dress shirt. He'd shed his sweater long before.

Selene stood next to Brenda, sleek and beautiful as always, in their Goth attire. Long, flowing black sweater layered over black skinny jeans and black boots. They wore a garnet necklace nestled among some longer silver chains.

They smelled of frankincense. Brenda inhaled the scent, grateful for it, wishing the younger person could actually do something to help. Wishing they were a powerhouse like Raquel, or even had Cassiel's sight.

"Can I make you some tea, Brenda? Or do anything else while we wait for Alejandro to work his magic?" Selene asked.

Brenda leaned into her coven mate for a moment, then sighed. "No, thank you, Selene. Nothing's going to calm me down right now."

Selene gave her a squeeze and went to sit next to Tobias, who was laying a Tarot spread out, trying to see if he could get information that way. That was a good place for them. Selene did know their cards.

Moss sat on Tobias's other side, sipping coffee, one foot crossed over his knee, shaking with impatience, or maybe nerves. He had a backward baseball cap on today, and looked so young to Brenda.

"Sit still, Moss," Tobias complained. Brenda walked toward Alejandro, and peered over his shoulder at the screen. The symbols scrolling by meant nothing to her. This was so not her sort of magic.

"Any luck?" Brenda finally asked him.

"Not yet. And I'm not sure I'll actually be able to do this. I'm not the hacker I used to be. Out of practice."

"But you'll keep trying?"

"I'll keep trying."

Brenda heard a commotion from the shop. A minute later, Tempest flung the curtain aside and Joshua from The Road Home rushed in.

"I got here as fast as I could! There were customers in the shop that wouldn't leave. I finally told them it was an emergency."

The younger man wore his usual fancy vest and sharply pressed slacks. No top hat today, though.

"What did I miss?" Joshua asked. He opened his arms, and Brenda walked into them, gratefully.

"Alejandro is trying to trace Caroline's phone, but so far he's not having any luck," Brenda spoke into Joshua's chest, then pulled back. "Caroline is in terrible danger, I can feel it. But I also have no idea how to find her."

"And you don't want to go to the police, why?" Joshua asked.

Brenda stepped all the way out of the circle of his arms and took up her pacing around the table again.

"First of all, not sure exactly what we tell them. I think I saw Rafe shove Caroline into a Lexus, but telling the police that a man may or may not have abducted his wife? They're not going to act on that right away anyway."

Tobias set down his cup of coffee and laced his hands behind his head. "Besides, Arrow and Crescent coven isn't exactly a favorite entity of the Portland Police Department. Not since we worked with my sweetie, Aiden, to get the sweeps stopped."

"And the chief came in, asking questions."

"What?" Moss said, slamming his go cup down on the table.

"It happened this morning, right after I opened. I told Tempest about it, then went for a short walk and saw Caroline getting stuffed inside a car. It kind of slipped my mind after that."

Joshua pulled out a chair and sat down. His posture was perfect, and he pulled down his cuffs. Topaz cufflinks winked at the bottom of his burgundy sleeves. She pulled out a chair and sat next to him, elbows on the table, face propped in her hands. She trained her eyes on his, and he matched her gaze, unflinchingly.

"Can you think of anything that might help?" she asked.

"Give me five minutes." Joshua slowly inhaled. Brenda felt the long pause after the inhalation and held her breath. And he exhaled just as slowly. Brenda matched her breath to him, recognizing the fourfold pattern. The long inhalation, followed by a pause. The long exhalation, a pause. It helped to calm her down, for which she was grateful.

As they breathed together, she tried to gather the ragged bits of her attention and her magic, back toward the central core she'd spent so many years building.

She could hear Tempest talking to some customers in

the shop, and the sound of Alejandro's fingers tapping keys. Following Joshua's lead, she let her awareness of everything going on around her to drop away. On her next breath, she shifted her attention onto the inner planes, hoping for insight, some vision of Caroline, or the answer they were seeking, of how in Diana's name they could help this woman.

:*Joshua knows.*: The Voice said.

How was it even back? She hadn't called it, but she felt it all the same, like a nimbus around her shoulders and head.

:*You needed me.*:

Okay then. She supposed that *had* been part of the deal: that if the angel had something of use to offer, it wasn't banished anymore.

Brenda had no choice but to trust that it was true. That this wasn't just a form of emotional wish fulfillment, or manipulation.

You better not mess this up, whatever you are. She shoved that thought, hard, toward the shaft of light she sensed around her back, then sank into her breathing once again.

Moss and Tobias conferred quietly together down at the other end of the table. In the space where her aura overlapped with Joshua's, Brenda felt a shift. It felt as though the air around his body became more palpable, and the atmosphere grew thicker. It was tangible.

"What's happening, Joshua?"

Alejandro's hands went still on the keyboard. Moss and Tobias stopped their conversation.

Joshua waved one hand in the air, eyes still closed, face looking sharp and intent. "Write this down."

"Got it," Alejandro said.

Joshua took in a deep breath. The pause afterward was so long, Brenda had to force herself to sit still, feet flat on the floor, palms held upright on her lap. She was treating herself as though she was one of her students. This was classic "how to keep centered and calm" posture. And one of the best ways to listen to a spirit when it was about to speak.

"The Angels have her well in hand." Joshua's voice was sonorous, deep and rich, more resonant than it usually was. It sounded as though he was speaking from a place that was both deep and far away. "Michael is with her. That much is clear. I see the river, and the edge of the freeway, a big steel bridge. The sound of the train."

Brenda leaned in close, careful not to disturb him. She pitched her voice low. "Which bridge, Joshua? Steel bridge? Hawthorne?"

His eyes fluttered behind the closed lids, and his breathing grew even deeper. The whole coven waited; not one person in the room moved. They were all well trained toward stillness and openness and listening for messages that came from wind or water or fire, or from the astral realms.

"There's warehouses. And I think...a fire station?"

"That's the east side of the Hawthorne Bridge," Moss said.

Brenda slid a hand across the table and gently placed her fingers on top of Joshua's. He gave a slight nod.

"But Caroline's okay?" Brenda asked.

"Yes. Michael is with her. The archangel." He took in a shuddering breath, withdrew his hand from hers, and shook himself. After one more long inhalation, he opened his eyes.

Moss was already on his feet, then crouching next to Joshua's chair. "Do you need anything? Tea? Some nuts to help you ground?"

Joshua shook his head. "I think we just need to go get

Caroline back. You're right, protein would be good after that. If you have them, I'll take some nuts to eat in the car."

Alejandro snapped his computer shut. "I can drive one of the cars," he said. "We'll need space for everyone here, plus room for Caroline."

"I'll drive," Moss said.

"Okay," Tobias said. "Do we need any supplies from the shop before we head out? Everyone got the tools they need?"

That was a good question, but one Brenda had no time for. She just needed to move. Grabbing her coat from the closet, she slipped her arms into the sleeves. She trusted her coven to gather whatever they needed, to get themselves ready to help her friend.

All Brenda could do? Was walk out the door, and try to keep herself from killing that man, Rafe.

And if it's necessary?

She'd cross that bridge when she came to it.

20

CAROLINE

A wind whipped itself up, throwing the rain in gusts against the car, flinging branches and leaves.

The rain and wind washed away the view of the river and the second train barreling past. The clanging warning bells and the flashing red lights were swept away by the power of water and air.

It felt as if the car was its own small world. A world of smooth, soft leather and expense. A world filled with the scent of drugs, burned skin, cologne, and fear.

A world where time alternately sped and slowed with the beating of her heart and the heaving of her breath.

Riding on the storm, she could hear the sound of wings.

Caroline fought her way over Rafe, trying to get to the door controls. She needed to unlock the damn car and get out. He wasn't making it easy, flailing at her with his shoulders, trying to keep his singed fingers out of the way.

"You bitch! What have you done?"

She honestly didn't know. This was the weirdest experience she'd ever had in her life. Getting the medallion had been strange enough. But the medallion burning Rafe's hands?

Thank you, Michael, for whatever it was you did.

"Where's the button?" she said, shoving her arms around him.

He heaved against her, pushing her back. The seatbelt snagged. Damn. Right. She had to get out of the seatbelt first. The handcuffs jangled between them, clattering into the footwell. No way was she letting him get those on her wrist again.

She shoved her hands between their bodies and felt for the end of the strap. There. Her fingers clicked the button and she was free.

The stench was growing worse. A miasma of scents. Caroline needed air. Real air.

"Let me out of the car, Rafe, or I'll burn the shit out of you again."

She would, too. She wasn't certain how, but she knew if she had to, she'd do it again. He didn't need to know it had been an accident. He just needed to be afraid.

Cradling his singed fingers, Rafe stared at her with wild, angry eyes.

"Where's the auto lock, Rafe?"

"Fuck you, bitch!"

He scrabbled for the bottle of water in the cup holder. "Damn it!" He couldn't grip the cap with his fingers. "Get this open!"

He was still so used to ordering her around.

Caroline grew still. "Open. The. Door. Rafe."

The wind howled and screamed outside. The beautiful spring sun long fled. The Pacific Northwest was showing the Californians who she really was.

Cutting through the sound of wind, Caroline heard the

rev of engines and the squeal of tires, then heavy doors slamming. Shouting. All of it a counterpoint to pouring rain. No time to look. She didn't dare to turn her head.

A pounding on the window. Someone shouting out her name. A man's voice. Deep and strong. She didn't know it. Then a voice she *did* know. A voice that sounded like the trumpet of an angel. Sweet. Fierce. Strong.

Brenda.

Freed from her seatbelt, Caroline launched herself across Rafe and pressed the unlock button. The locks *chunked* up and the passenger door opened. She felt hands on her shoulders, pulling her out into the rain. Strong arms grabbed her waist; another arm, gentler, wrapped around her arms.

"Caroline, thank the Goddess!"

"It's you," Caroline said, turning toward the voice. Blue, blue eyes. Silver crescents dangling from the pale lobes of her ears. Wisps of dark hair plastered to her face by rain. Lipstick the color of cherries, half bitten off her lips.

Caroline breathed in the scent of her. The Brenda-ness of her. She was dimly aware of Rafe's voice, still bellowing, answered sharply by other voices.

All she cared about was that Brenda had come to get her, the light of an angel hovering around her shoulders.

"Let's get her into one of the cars, okay?" A man's voice cut through. She turned her head. He was handsome, with deeply tanned skin. Looked like a businessman. Caroline realized he was the one with the arms around her waist.

Bam! Something slammed into them. The man's arms tightened, then Caroline was picked up and swung to the side, out of the way. He let her go. Caroline stumbled against Brenda, who snatched her arms and pulled her toward one of the waiting cars.

Caroline whirled to see Rafe, head and shoulders buried in the businessman's chest. The man struggled to control him, but Rafe kept pushing, bellowing.

There were more people around, grabbing at the men, tugging at them, trying to pull them apart.

The rain battered her face. The wind roared in her ears. Sound stretched outward. The droplets of rain seemed huge, fat, and slow. A leaf floated by. Light strobed at the edges of Caroline's eyes. Then there was a flash. Then gray.

Then nothing but the sense of falling against something soft, and something hard.

A light. A voice.

:*Be not afraid.*:

I'm not. But...what's happening?

:*You will be well. Just trust now.*:

Trust.

Caroline coughed and blinked, then realized the soft thing she had fallen against was Brenda, and the woman was cradling her head in her lap, stroking her hair off her face. Brenda was bent around her, protecting her from the rain.

She was so beautiful. She felt like home.

"Thank you," Caroline mouthed, not sure if any sound even came out. The rain and wind still roared, and voices shouted. Close. Too close.

She turned her head and saw a well-dressed Latinx businessman, and a scruffy woman with strands of wet dark hair flying around her head, and a young white man—kicking the shit out of Rafe.

Caroline looked back up at Brenda. Joshua loomed over Brenda's shoulder. It was clear he'd been pouring energy into her. They were both keeping her protected.

"Stop them," Caroline said.

Joshua just nodded and stepped toward the scrum, reaching in among the flailing limbs, putting hands on shoulders, and pulling them away from Rafe, who huddled on the tarmac, head cradled in his hands.

Caroline fought to sit up. Brenda helped her, still cradling her, offering support to her back. Her head pounded and her mouth was dry as dust despite the water everywhere. She just wanted to go to sleep.

She just wanted this done.

The man and woman dragged Rafe upright. He stumbled, then caught himself. The palms of his hands looked raw, as if layers of skin had been burned away.

"Do you want us to call the police?" the man holding one of Rafe's arms asked her.

Caroline considered. Did she? She felt the fluttering of wings and the warmth of light behind her. What would happen if she pressed charges? What would happen to her life?

She would have to return to Silicon Valley. She would have to face her family and what friends she had.

She would maybe need to face a trial.

Caroline didn't want to go through any of that. She wanted justice, but she also wanted a life as far away from him as she could get. Pressing charges would bind her against him more tightly, until he what? Went to prison for a couple of years? Paid a fine?

No. She needed a more permanent solution.

"I want you to do magic to make him stop. And I want the angels to protect me. And Rafe? I never want to see you again."

21

BRENDA

The spring storm had landed with a vengeance. Equinox was on its way, but it felt closer to winter than summer outside.

Wind smacked against the attic window and shook the mighty trees outside Raquel's home.

Beeswax candles scented the peak-ceilinged room, blending with the smells of white sage and balsam. The ghost of frankincense and myrrh always perfumed the air, but the other smells overpowered them today.

Brenda was worried sick about Caroline, and wanted to be with her, but Caroline had specifically asked that she be here.

"I need your magic," she had said, as Brenda held her close in the back seat of Alejandro's car. So here Brenda was, keeping a promise to a woman she was rapidly falling in love with. A woman she barely knew, but who had somehow caught ahold of a corner of her soul.

Brenda was filled with rage that anyone had dared to harm Caroline. It tasted like metal on her tongue.

Brenda wanted to lash out, to hurl as much baneful

magic at that man as she could muster, but cooler heads had prevailed. Raquel had been particularly insistent, and was right, as usual. Brenda wasn't thinking clearly, and that was bad for any operation, especially one as important as this.

So it had been decided. Selene was in charge of the ritual tonight tonight. The coven had agreed that they had the most clarity of vision around what needed to happen. Besides, Selene was the best at making poppets, which was the major part of tonight's work.

Tempest sat next to Brenda, teal hair clipped back off her face. She sent soothing energy toward Brenda through warm hands. It went a long way toward calming her down.

"Thank you," Brenda murmured.

Tempest replied with a small smile, and just kept on. She was truly a master healer, the best the coven had, and that was saying something, because some of the others were very gifted.

Selene was in the center, throwing more herbs onto charcoal, gathering the red twine, the lemon, the pins, and the lock of Rafe's hair that Moss had the foresight to rip from the man's head in the middle of the parking lot fight.

Brenda's thoughts kept going to Caroline, who she hoped was being taken care of by her friends. Lucy, Alejandro, and Moss had set up wards around Sydney and Dan's home when they dropped Caroline there. She should be safe enough.

Brenda had never wanted to kill anyone in her whole life, but she wanted to kill Rafe.

So the coven was in Raquel's attic, behind every ward and protection they could erect around the space. Arrow and Crescent was ready to call upon Diana to send out her hounds and to do what needed to be done to find and bind the man.

Archangel Michael had already seen to his punishment. The coven just needed to make sure he wouldn't do anything like this again.

Brenda shoved a cushion behind her back and leaned against the knee wall behind her.

"Are you almost ready?" Moss asked Selene.

They nodded, and swept the straight fall of black hair over their shoulder. Selene looked serious, almost grim. Garnet winked around Selene's neck, matching the color of their broad lips. Selene turned their dark eyes on Brenda, as though asking for permission.

Brenda gave a tight nod, barely able to move her head. When had she grown so tense? Tempest ran her soothing hands across Brenda's shoulders, and down her arms, flicking her fingers at the end, as though casting off evil spirits. Sending the discordant energies away.

Brenda sighed with relief, then realized the whole coven was looking toward her. Her friends, her mentors, her peers.

Lucy, who was always so steady and strong. Alejandro, the businessman, the wizard to Brenda's witch. Moss, ready to leap into the fray the minute justice was threatened anywhere. Tobias, the other healer in the group, the one she had mentored herself. Cassiel, who was finally growing into her powers.

And of course, Tempest and Raquel. Brenda's student, and her best friend.

:*They are the ones you have waited your whole life to find. They are those who journeyed far and wide, for lifetime after lifetime, to work with you again.*:

And the Voice. Angel or demon, Brenda guessed it was here to stay for a while. She still hoped she would figure out why it had shown up and what was wrong. When a big power like that arrived all of a sudden, it usually was a signal that something bad was about to go down.

Or that your life was going to change in a big way.

Initiation, her own inner voice said again. Well, she didn't want to hear that, did she? *Piss off,* she thought.

Before getting to her problems, or any of the other weird stuff going on, the coven needed to deal with this particular bad thing first. Brenda didn't need to know how or if Caroline's husband was connected with the voices the police chief, and Brenda, and all those people seeking out the Inner Eye were hearing.

Deal with the proximate situation first, then figure out the pattern.

She didn't like to work that way. She always preferred to get to the larger picture first, but Caroline needed help, and she needed it now.

Dealing with Rafe couldn't wait.

"Please," she said. "Start when you're ready."

Selene gestured to Raquel, who stood to speak.

"We are here to bear witness. We are here to ensure protection for one who needs it. We are here to set a binding on one who has harmed others and may yet harm himself. We ask our inner wisdom to rise up and fill each of us, so we know the correct actions to take tonight to mete out justice, and no more. We invoke our deepest selves, asking for guidance. May the best possible outcome be spun."

Brenda's breath slowed as her friend was speaking, and she could feel each coven member around her slowing down and sinking into themselves, ready to do magic.

Selene raised both their arms, silver and leather bracelets cascading down their wrist bones, pushing back the black sleeves of their shirt.

"Diana!" they called. "Be with us! Guide my mind, my

heart, my hands. Let your magic run true through my blood as I bind this man, Rafe, from harming this woman, Caroline, and from harming anyone else, including himself. May we do this work in your name, to ensure that any inevitable pain is minimized, and that the processes of healing become possible over time."

Brenda felt the power of the words ripple through the space. She trusted Selene to unravel the necessary threads and to bind Rafe from doing further harm in as limited a fashion as they could.

Which was why Brenda wasn't in charge. The way she felt right now? She'd tie the man up and set him on fire.

The wind moaned outside, whipping across the rooftops. Raquel's ritual space felt warm, secure. Like home.

Sink into that, Brenda. And let Selene do their work.

Selene was carving symbols onto the lemon skin with a porcupine quill, adding the sharp, clearing scent of citrus to the blend of smells in the attic space.

Setting the quill aside, they picked up the hank of hair and the red thread, beginning the process of binding the hair to the lemon. They wound the red thread around and around the fruit, muttering a chant as they went, rocking back and forth, raising energy. Brenda could feel the magic sparking through Selene's fingertips, wreathing the red thread, encasing the citrus with power.

The energy in the room shifted as every coven member focused attention on Selene, feeding them power. Every coven member except Tempest and Brenda. Brenda still did not trust herself to not mess up the working, and Tempest was there to steady her. It was good. This working needed to be clean. Clear. Strong.

The winding of the thread was done.

Selene picked up six straight pins, and passed them, one

by one, through a candle flame. She pushed one through the top of the lemon's flesh, and another through the bottom. The remaining four formed an equator around the central line of the fruit.

Brenda could feel the thread, the hair, the lemon. She felt the energy as the pins locked into place, all aiming toward the heart of the lemon.

Selene raised the fruit up toward the attic peak. "Brothers and sisters, siblings, family! Witches, hear me now! Powers ancient and wise! Powers of the the Elemental Forces! Ancestors! Gods! Goddesses! Attend!"

The air felt thick, and throbbed with power. Brenda's spine snapped upright. The edges of her skin stood at attention.

"Diana! Send your hounds to find this man, Rafe! May his spirit and flesh be bound from committing more harm! May he see his error. May he seek out change."

Selene's voice grew silent. A candle flame snapped. The wind and rain still blew outside. Brenda heard her own breath, entering and exiting her lungs.

Selene passed their right hand over the lemon, three times.

"And if he refuses to see his error, if this man Rafe seeks once again to harm"—their voice grew as harsh as the wind —"may he know terror unceasing, from now until such a time as he buckles, weeping, to his knees. Then offer him a vision of the way his life could be. Let it not be said you are unmerciful, our Lady. Let every human being always choose their path."

Selene dropped their hands then, and sagged just a little as the power left them. Their shining black hair became a curtain around their face.

Moss and Raquel rushed forward. Raquel wrapped a

blanket around Selene's back, and Moss gently took the bound-up fruit from their hands. He laid it on top of a piece of foil, and carefully wrapped it, until it was completely encased in a sheath of aluminum.

"The working is done," Selene croaked out. "And I need a cup of tea."

They gave a sharp bark of laughter. "Or maybe a glass of wine."

"We have both of those ready," Tobias said. "I'll be right back." He opened the attic door. Brenda could hear him padding down the stairs.

She scooted her way to the center of the circle and opened her arms. Brenda had never felt as close to Selene as she did to some of the other coven members, but after that piece of magic, every part of her wanted to hold Selene close. To rock them. To thank them for doing what she herself had not been able to do.

Selene smiled at Brenda, even paler than usual, and, still wrapped in the soft teal blanket, snuggled her head onto Brenda's shoulders and waited for Tobias to return with tea and wine.

Thank you, Diana. And thank you to everyone else who helped tonight.

She just hoped Caroline was going to be all right. And that Rafe would stay away. If he could combat a binding that strong, the coven might be in big trouble.

:*You have allies.*:

Usually that was a good thing, but the allies—if that was what they were—that were gathering around them all these days?

They only made Brenda feel more afraid.

22

CAROLINE

I t was growing late, but Caroline didn't want to go to bed yet. She was exhausted, but still keyed up from the kidnapping and assault.

At the insistence of Sydney, Caroline was ensconced on the well-stuffed leather sofa in the living room, Bella's head resting next to her thigh. She rested, legs tucked up under the soft blue-and-burgundy weave of a throw blanket. A cooling cup of tea was close at hand on the coffee table.

Caroline had a headache.

It almost felt as though she had the dregs of a hangover —not that she'd had one of those since college—or as if she was coming down with the flu. Brenda's friend Raquel told her she would likely feel ill for a while. It was the aftermath of everything she'd been through with Rafe—the fear, the heightened adrenaline—added to whatever the heck was going on with that angel. Archangel, she corrected herself. Michael.

Her fingers touched the medal at her breastbone for a moment, as if to reassure herself it was still there. Amazingly, it hadn't been ripped from her neck in the struggle.

The coven had dropped her at Sydney and Dan's home, then done some sort of magic to protect the place before they left. Brenda had kissed her gently on the lips before walking to the car.

She stretched, and slid further down the couch. Sydney and Dan's home was comfortable, that was for sure; much as it had been hard to watch Brenda leave, she felt comforted here. Comfortable. And she knew the coven was doing what they could to make sure she stayed safe.

Caroline touched her lips, remembering the kiss. Caroline still didn't fully trust her feelings for Brenda. They were too strong. Too sudden.

But she came for you, Caroline thought. *When you needed her, she was there.*

And with backup, too. Caroline wasn't sure what to think of all of that, either. Not yet. But it looked as though she'd have a few days to ponder it, at least. She was going to have to call her parents and let them know what was happening. And get the wheels turning on a divorce.

That last thought kindled a sense of vague excitement. Possibility. It also made her tense up again. She didn't need to think of it. Not now.

There was so much to be done, but Caroline was still tired. Brenda had just called to report that the magical working was done. Caroline had wanted to ask all about it, but Brenda sounded exhausted herself, and said she'd get a full report later.

"Get some rest," Brenda had said before ringing off. Caroline was trying.

The yellow lab sighed, and Caroline scratched her head. Sydney had encouraged the dog to lie down on the floor beneath the coffee table. It was nice. Caroline had never lived with a dog before.

Pulling the blanket around her shoulders, she settled more deeply against the plump cushion behind her back. A small fire warmed the grate, birch logs popping and perfuming the air.

Caroline stared at the dance of the flames in the hearth, and absently petted Bella's head. The rains lashed at the large windows, and wind still whirled and moaned through the mighty elms outside.

Portland was filled with trees. They made her feel safe, somehow. Sheltered.

Her body felt bruised, and her muscles were strained in unusual ways. But when she thought about it, she realized her spirit felt good. Better than it had for a long time.

Things had felt...different after Brenda called, saying the coven was done. It was as though the tension that had become a constant in Caroline's life had dissipated. It wasn't gone yet, she supposed that would take time, but she actually felt as if she could breathe again.

Dan poked his head out of the kitchen. "Can I get you some more tea?"

She looked up at Dan and smiled, "That'd be great."

Caroline knew he wanted to help. She could also tell he was a little bit freaked out by the situation, but trying not to let on. Sydney walked back into the room, reading glasses perched on the end of her nose, staring at her phone.

"I'll do more research," she said. "But so far, it's looking as though there are several support groups for survivors of domestic violence." Sydney took her glasses off and folded them into the pocket of her sweater.

It was so good to see her old friend that Caroline practically ached with it. She hadn't realized how much Rafe had isolated her. Really, the only people she saw were Rafe and her parents. And then the people at the gem shows. She loved the trade shows, as much for the rocks and gemstones, as for the chance to interact with like-minded people, because she never got the chance, otherwise. How had she not realized that?

"You're beating yourself up again, aren't you?" Sydney sat in a comfortable, blue suede chair. "None of this is your fault."

Caroline balked at that. "Don't you believe that once we're adults we have to take some responsibility for our lives?

"Yes. But you *do*. And you know you do. But abuse like this? You *can't* blame yourself. It's a form of slow brainwashing. The changes are incremental, and by the time a person realizes it, the pattern is set, and things are so far gone it's hard to escape."

Caroline sighed and sipped her tepid tea. Ginger and mint. It eased some of the aching in her head. "How do you know so much about this?"

"I've spent enough time doing pro bono work for abused women that I've had to research all sorts of things. Won a lot of cases, by the way. Give me a minute and we can talk about it some more. I'm going to get some wine. Do you want some?"

Caroline gingerly shook her head. "No, the witches all said I need to stick with tea for a day or two."

The two women smiled at one another. "Those witches sound like wise women. I look forward to spending more time with them." Dan was just coming out of the kitchen, and they exchanged a small kiss as they passed. Dan poured fresh tea from a small green pot, the steam fragrant and warm on Caroline's cheeks.

"Thanks," she said.

Dan set the pot on a coaster on the coffee table, then sat

in the second chair and slung his feet up onto an embroidered ottoman. Turning his head, he called into the kitchen, "Would you bring me a glass too, love?"

She and Rafe had never had that. There was passion and heat, sure, which over the years had shifted more and more from sex and into anger, but they'd never had this easy companionability. There was never a sense of home.

It felt good here. She loved this place. She was liking Portland so far, but she loved watching Sydney and Dan, and the life they built together.

"Your home feels so...homey." She smiled at her remark. "I know that sounds strange, and kind of dumb...."

"It doesn't," Dan said. "We worked hard on it. Right, Bella?" The dog raised her head and looked at Dan, then plopped her head back down on the edge of the couch. Caroline scratched behind the dog's silky ears again. Bella sighed in contentment.

"Sydney and I decided what we wanted out of life, and set about building it. We've been fortunate enough that we've been able to do so." He gestured around the room at the furniture, the fireplace, the dog. "This is the result. I try never to take it for granted."

Sydney came back in from the kitchen, a glass of red wine in each hand. "We are fortunate indeed," she said.

"What do you mean by that?" Caroline said. "You've used that word before."

Sydney sipped at her wine, thinking. "Well, it isn't just luck, though luck plays a big part in it. And it's not just our privilege, though that's included, too. It's some combination of circumstance, luck, and work. We wouldn't have all of this if any one of those had been missing. That's fortune."

Maybe Caroline's fortune was changing. Something had given her the courage to smash that tracker and head north.

And something had enabled her to fight Rafe for the first time in their relationship. She didn't even realize she was *deciding*; she just found herself *doing*.

Almost as though they responded to her thoughts, the amethyst point and the angel medallion warmed and began to hum again. Caroline felt a ray of light surround her heart. It felt like the light she'd seen around Brenda's head and shoulders.

She took a sip of tea, trying to buy herself time. To take it all in. She had angels now, and whether they came in the form of a shopkeeper, a coven of witches, or actual beings made of swan wings and light, it didn't seem to matter. What was clear was that her life was going to be different now, if she decided it was going to be.

Whether she'd ever assimilate these changes, she wasn't sure, but damn it, Caroline was determined to not go back to Silicon Valley, and to Rafe, and to hiding in the shadows. Never again.

"Are you okay?" Sydney asked.

"Well, I can't deny that this is all strange, and a little bit scary. But it also feels right, you know? I feel as though for the first time in my life..." She paused, searching for the words. "For the first time in my life, I think I'm ready to be free."

Dan raised his wineglass, and Sidney did the same. They both waited, looking at her, until she raised her mug of tea.

"To the possibility of freedom," Dan said.

"To freedom," Caroline said

To freedom, she thought. *And maybe even love.*

23

BRENDA

The windstorm finally calmed down, leaving behind leaf-clogged streets and rain. Corvus Corax was playing their medieval music over the sound system at the Inner Eye; the scent of myrrh and lavender filled the air.

Brenda was weary, and confused. It was strange. She hadn't felt confused like this in years. Confused about her magic, about the coven, about this shaft of light that was following her around. About Caroline, though she was less confused about that every day. Even though she'd just met the woman, and barely spent any time with her, it was clear that she wanted to. Badly.

That said, Brenda never thought she'd reach the age of forty-one questioning so many things at once.

She dusted the shelves, keeping an eye on the couple of customers in the store. *I've been a mentor and a teacher for years,* she thought. *Why all this, and why now?*

Thrust into a situation where the coven actually had to curse and bind someone... That was happening more and more lately. She wondered if it was because they were well-trained enough now. She and Raquel had worked hard to get the coven to this place, but neither of them had expected it would lead to the sorts of magic they been doing the past few months.

Stability meant power, and power meant meant more responsibility. *You say that to your students all the time*, she thought. She said a lot of things, even meant them. And now she just had to find the ways in which those truths and maxims were coming to play in her own life.

Her throat felt raw, and she hoped she wasn't coming down with a cold. The stress and tension of the week, of rescuing Caroline...of kneeling in that parking lot in the howling wind and rain, protecting the woman who had collapsed in her arms.

She had wanted nothing more than to keep her safe. Brenda had held Caroline in her arms for a long time, body hunched over her, rocking her gently. She'd barely paid attention as the rest of the coven took care of Rafe. He had kicked and fought, until they finally subdued him, and Caroline had said she didn't want the police called in.

And before they had arrived, it was clear Caroline had done something, too.

Lucy said there were strange burns on his fingers. That even as he fought them, he kept trying to protect his hands.

Brenda needed to ask Caroline what had happened. What she'd done. There'd been too much to do the night before, so they hadn't had a chance to talk. Maybe Brenda could see stop by to see her tonight, after work.

The bells over the shop door jangled and Brenda looked up. A well-dressed, middle-aged Black woman walked through, hair perfectly coiffed despite the rain. She slid her umbrella into the stand just inside the door. A long, red raincoat was buttoned up all the way to a beautiful red-and-purple patterned scarf that twined around the woman's neck. She looked vaguely familiar, though Brenda couldn't say where she might've seen her.

Brenda smiled. "Just let me know if you need anything," she said, before turning back to the display of Buddhist statuary she was dusting.

The woman walked directly towards her, high heeled pumps striking the bamboo floors. Brenda straightened and turned to face her.

"Are you the proprietor?"

"I am. My name is Brenda." She held out her hand. The woman hesitated for one moment, then held out her own. As soon as Brenda touched her fingertips, she understood the hesitation. Something was very, very wrong. Brenda let go and looked around the store. Tempest was helping someone with the crystals; another person browsed some divination tools. Brenda didn't want to sit in chairs near the book section, that was too open.

She led the woman back to the nook where she did readings.

"Let's go sit down," Brenda said over her shoulder. "It's clear you have a lot going on. We'll see if I can be of any help."

The woman's shoulders slumped a bit, in relief. She followed Brenda to the cozy little table and two chairs tucked into an alcove. As soon as they were seated, Brenda pulled out one of the Tarot decks that was always in a basket on the table. She slid the deck from its silk bag and started flipping through the cards. They felt right in her hands, cool and smooth. The energy began to gather, the way it always did when she was about to do a reading.

The woman hadn't asked her for a reading, not yet. But Brenda knew better than to question her impulses when it came to magic. She wasn't a psychic for nothing. This, she wasn't confused about at all.

Brenda looked at the woman's face. She was very beautiful, with smooth dark skin and a narrow nose that flared out around the nostrils. Her lips were painted a deep mulberry. Her eyes looked terrified, and furrows marred her brow.

"Why don't you tell me what's going on?"

The woman looked around, making sure no one was close enough to hear. She leaned towards Brenda. "I've been having dreams," she said. "And...and there've been voices."

Brenda's hands stilled around the cards. Not the voices, not again.

:*Trust this, too. Seek the pattern, find the light,*: the Voice said.

I keep hoping you'll leave, she thought.

:*I am the messenger of all that is,*: the voice replied.

Yeah, yeah. One more thing to deal with.

She addressed the woman, who kept playing with her hands, first clasping them together, then pulling them apart.

"I want you to know that I hear and see many things that people think are strange. And I've heard and seen enough of them that I know they aren't."

"You can't tell me this stuff is normal."

"Maybe *normal* isn't the right word, but dreams, visions, even voices, are not uncommon. What are they telling you?"

The woman held her fingers to her lips for a moment, and swallowed. She wouldn't hold Brenda's gaze. That was fine, give her time.

"They're terrible," she whispered. "Women. Young girls. They're all terrified. Screaming. They're being raped. Tortured." The woman darted her eyes up at Brenda, then back down at the table. "And they want something from me."

Brenda's fingers started shuffling the deck again. The cards slipped and slid against one another. The diamond-patterned back of the deck winked in and out among the brightly colored images. Here was the Devil. The ten of swords. Three of swords, piercing the heart. The ace of wands. Temperance. All of them sliding past, moving beneath her hands, like the old friends that they were.

"And what do you think they want from you?" Brenda asked.

"I don't know! Well...I..."

"Take your time."

"They keep asking me to help them. But I don't know how."

That sounded right to Brenda, but it didn't feel as though it was the whole story. Something else was going on here.

"Are you sure you don't know how to help?" The woman did look at her this time, dead on. Fear and anger warred for precedence on her face.

"How am I supposed to help them? I don't even know who they are! Or if they're even real."

The light surrounded Brenda then. She felt it, as though someone had wrapped a warm sweater around her shoulders. The cards slipped and slid, slid and slipped, snapping beneath her fingers as she switched to a classic poker shuffle.

She tapped the cards. Shuffled again. The air buzzed with power.

"Close the curtains," she said, not stopping.

She felt the woman rise, heard the soft clatter of curtain rings on the rod, felt the alcove grow closer. More intimate. The power built. The sense of the light increased.

Finally, the cards stilled beneath her hands. "Touch the deck," Brenda said. "And say a prayer to whomever you usually call on. Ask for their help, and for the cards to show us what we need to know."

The woman slid her hands across the table, and Brenda placed them gently on the deck. The woman bowed her head. When she raised it again, Brenda saw that she still looked frightened, but also ready for whatever messages were about to come through.

And come through they would. Brenda could feel the information pushing at her skin, ready to burst forth. If the cards hadn't been so insistent on playing their part, Brenda could have just read the woman with no props, no tools, with nothing but the taste and scent of the air between them, and the thoughts shimmering and racing behind the woman's eyes.

But the cards must have their say.

"Cut them into three piles, and choose which pile goes back on top."

Once she was done, Brenda took the deck and began to lay out the cards.

High Priestess, reversed. A woman on a throne, crowned with a crescent moon, sitting between black and white pillars, a scroll on her lap.

The three of swords again. The long blades piercing a heart.

Ten of swords. Waking from a nightmare.

Justice reversed. The scales, balancing.

The Ace of Wands. A single club. A torch. Clarity of purpose.

Seven of cups. Confusion. Illusion. Delusion.

Judgment. The dead, rising to the sound of Gabriel's trumpet.

"Who are you?" Brenda whispered. Before the woman could respond, she held up a hand. "Wait. Don't answer that. It's all around you. The images. The story."

She tapped the cards. "There is a person with a broken heart who thinks she is a priestess, holding the scroll of wisdom. But the broken heart is driving her forward. The priestess is unbalanced, reversed. So whatever justice she seeks is also reversed. Whatever she does, her actions don't have the desired effect. She is prey to delusion. Desperation. But her soul is on fire with the truth. What she wants is true, but everything around her is confused."

Brenda was barely reading the cards at all. She simply used the imagery they provided to tell the story forming inside her head, as the words tumbled from her lips. She rocked slightly, forward and back, as the energies in the small alcove increased.

"This woman is sending you the nightmares. And the voices you hear are the voices of traumatized women, seeking justice. Whoever this person is, she is the one behind it all. Do you know who she is?"

Tears ran down the woman's face and her body shook. Her breath came in small pants. An acrid scent hit Brenda's nose. The woman's fear, seeping from her pores.

"I don't know," she said. And Brenda knew with a flash the woman across the table was lying.

"I asked before, but now I want to know. Who are you?"

The woman gasped, then swallowed, hard.

"I am..." She cleared her throat and tried again. "I am Judge Anita Ratner, U.S. District Court."

:*She is the key.*:

"Well, judge, someone from your past surely wants your attention. And a whole lot of women want to have their say."

Brenda swept the cards back together, and began to shuffle them into the larger deck.

"I'd ask yourself what case you heard where a woman was wronged and didn't get justice."

24

CAROLINE

I t felt too soon to be going to a meeting like this.

The church function room was pleasant enough, Caroline supposed. Formica floor, cold fluorescent lights. An industrial coffeepot set up on a table against the white wall. A corkboard was covered in posters about worship services and concerts, fliers for meetings, and next to it hung a big, inspirational collage that read "Healing is always possible."

She'd never been in a place like this, but she supposed it was typical. She had certainly read enough about them, and seen people standing outside of churches talking. She always figured they were waiting for their AA or Al-Anon meeting to begin.

And now here she was, a woman who hadn't set foot in a church since her own wedding years ago, at her first domestic abuse survivors meeting. She sat in an uncomfortable, molded plastic chair, one in a circle of fourteen or so. Other women drifted in, and some men, too, which surprised her. Maybe it shouldn't. Anybody could be a victim, she supposed. It just seemed that women bore the brunt of it.

Two women greeted a man over by the coffee pot. Friendly. As if they'd known each other for a long time. As if they knew the drill. Others, like her, headed straight for the chairs, shucked off their raincoats, and sat, scrolling through phones, or closing their eyes for a few moments' rest before the meeting was called to order.

Caroline held a cardboard coffee cup in her hands. It looked watery and didn't smell very good. The only creamer was the powdered kind, which she hated. Besides, her head still felt funny, and she wasn't sure if she should start back on caffeine so soon.

She'd gotten the coffee just to have something to do. Caroline wasn't a hundred percent sure why she was here, except that Sydney and Brenda both thought it might be a good idea, so after tea and conversation with Sydney and Dan, Caroline had driven herself here.

Brenda said she would try to meet her for dinner this evening. Caroline hoped she could.

They'd all deemed Caroline safe enough, now that the binding was done and her old phone was gone. Alejandro had taken care of that, disabling it, clearing its memory. Getting it ready to be passed along to someone else who needed it. Her new phone was clean, he insisted. Untraceable unless someone got into the hardware directly. *Rafe* certainly couldn't trace her phone again. She was no longer on the family plan that had given him access in the first place. The bastard.

You're done with him now, she told herself. Except she wasn't. There was still a divorce to get through. Meetings with lawyers. Injunctions. Luckily, she had her business account, and was glad she had slowly syphoned small amounts of cash into it, month after month. Fortune.

Rafe hadn't noticed the slow accrual, because he'd never seen the money in the first place. As long as she put enough money into their joint account to pay the bills, he let her run her business on her own. He never knew how much she made from her "hobby."

Caroline wished she could have seen Brenda this morning, and felt a little crestfallen that Brenda had to work, but she also knew it was time to take the reins of her life into her own hands. Maybe this meeting was the start of that, or maybe it wasn't. It didn't really matter, she realized. She just had to try.

A woman with blond, curly hair and ample hips sat next to her. Caroline looked up and gave her half a smile, not sure what the protocol was here, and not really certain she wanted to talk to anybody.

"My name is Sharon." The woman held out a hand, silver rings on two fingers. Caroline shook it, reluctantly. There was something slightly off about the woman. She had the feel of an old-timer about her, the same feeling Caroline got from the people still in conversation at the coffee pot. As though she'd been coming here for a long time. But that wasn't what was off. There was something…brittle about her. And a strange, hectic look danced around her hazel eyes.

"Caroline," she finally responded.

"First time?"

"Yeah. I'm not sure if I'll stay. But some friends suggested I check it out. See if it might help me."

Sharon fussed with a heavy, red leather purse, dragging out her phone and checking something before putting it away again. Caroline caught a glimpse of something that look like the stack of papers as she rummaged through the leather monstrosity. Flyers? The woman paused, noticed her glance, and pulled out one of the sheets.

Sure enough, it was a small, postcard-sized flyer.

"Well, you won't get any justice here, that's for sure, or in the courts," Sharon said. "I didn't, with my husband. And my sweet daughter certainly didn't, three years ago, after her rape. But at least you'll find some people who might understand what you're going through. Sometimes that's all we get, you know?"

Caroline *didn't* know. But she felt like she shouldn't say anything. Caroline just wanted to get her own life in order, not help a bunch of other people. Maybe coming to this meeting was a mistake.

"If you're interested, here's a flyer about a project I've been working on for the past four years."

The woman held out the small sheet of white paper. An offering. The black lines of printing looked strange to Caroline's eyes. It was as though they were moving, and had a life of their own. She hoped that wasn't because of the headache that was still a dull presence in the back of her skull.

There was no way she could refuse the paper without giving offense, so she took it. She was going to have to train herself to not care about offending people, Caroline supposed. But perhaps today was not that day.

"Thanks."

The flier looked as off as the woman who had it made. *"The winds of change will blow your house down!"* it read in large bold letters across the longer side. *"The halls of justice are the halls of shame,"* the next line read. Then the type grew smaller. Caroline skimmed it. It looked like some treatise on the incompetence of the local police and court systems.

Caroline had no idea why the woman thought she would be interested.

She noticed that her pendant had grown warm against her chest again. She grasped it between her thumb two fingers.

Michael? she thought. *What's going on?*

She realize the woman was still talking to her, voice pitched low.

"...and if you're interested, I've been doing magic about this. The cops, the courts, none of them were any help in my daughter's case. So I've been taking justice into my own hands."

"How are you doing that?" The words were out of Caroline's mouth before she could call them back. *Great, Caroline, now you have this unhinged woman talking to you about magic. This is the last thing you need.*

The woman leaned in closer. Carolyn caught an old cigarette scent from her red–and-black sweater coat. That was funny, who even smoked anymore? Sharon smelled of menthol, like the stuff your mother rubbed on your chest when you had a cough. The combination of that with the stale cigarette smell was making Caroline feel queasy. All of a sudden, she was back in the car with Rafe pinning her to the seat, breathing into her mouth.

Her heartbeat increased its tempo. She was starting to sweat.

And she really didn't want to be here anymore.

"So I've been haunting them."

Haunting them? What the hell did that mean?

The woman's eyes really looked wild now. They sparked and flashed. Her tongue darted out, just for an instance, then was gone again. "I sent voices into their heads. You can help me. I know you can. You have *him*, he's very strong. He can help us too."

Caroline realized the woman was pointing to her Archangel Michael medal. *No,* she thought. *Not him. You can't have him.*

Clutching the flyer in her hand, Caroline gathered up her own slim black bag, grabbed her coat from the back of the hard plastic chair, and stood.

"I'm sorry, I don't feel very well all of a sudden. I think I need to leave." Caroline fled through the church doors, back out into the lightly falling rain.

She needed to see Brenda. She needed to see her now.

25

BRENDA

Brenda was closing up the shop. Tempest was already gone—she'd had a lot of massage clients booked for the afternoon.

Brenda was fortunate that her coven mate was able to staff the Inner Eye at all, and that it worked with her schedule. Brenda didn't mind being alone in the shop. She actually liked it.

Except on weekends, the shop was generally just busy enough to keep the business in the black, but not so busy that one person couldn't handle things on their own. She kept hoping to be able to hire someone else, but it hadn't worked out so far.

She was re-shelving some books, and the shop was actually empty for the first time all day. Her thoughts were on the judge. And the police chief. And the random customer, weeping in the book section, wanting to kill herself.

All of them hearing voices, telling them seriously bad things.

Brenda barely noticed the violin piping through the shop, except that she was glad for the music. Lindsay Sterling, Tempest had said it was. The bells over the door chimed, and then clanged as the door shut again. Damn. She'd hoped to get out of here before seeing anyone else. After dealing with that judge, she needed time to think. And maybe consult with Raquel.

Brenda set her stack of books back onto the low table between the two comfortable reading chairs. It was the young man, the one who would come in asking about Palo Santo and then run off. The one the Voice had told her carried light, and needed protection.

His windbreaker had given way to an army duffle coat, with a fake-fur-lined hood. The Chuck Taylors were replaced by purple Doc Marten boots.

"Welcome back," she said. He looked a little sheepish at that, but smiled.

"Yeah," he drawled out, "think I got a little spooked. But something told me I needed to talk to you."

"Come have a seat while I re-shelve these books."

"I can help if you like," the young man said

There was a tingling around Brenda's head, and a flash of light. Whether it was the young man or the angel, she had a good feeling about this one. There was something about him. Whether he was a psychic like her, or an empath, or just had a propensity toward magic, she was glad he had returned.

She caught a wave of relief, mingled with worry. Empath, then. He likely caught as well as projected emotions. He definitely needed to work on that if he was going to survive in this world.

He took off his jacket and draped it over one of the chairs, careful to keep the rainy side off the upholstery. A green cardigan with leather elbow patches topped today's T-shirt. *Unlocking the Truth*, the shirt said. If that was a band,

Brenda had never heard of them, but she couldn't help but be intrigued by the name.

"It should be pretty self-explanatory, but if you run into trouble, just ask me where they go." Brenda put a small stack of books into his waiting arms. "So, what brings you here on this drizzly night?"

"After I left the other day," he said, "what you said stayed with me. But more than that, it was the feeling I got when I was here."

They shelved books in silence for a moment, accompanied by the sound the rain, the violin, and cars shushing by. Two women's voices laughing together, rose and fell as they headed down the sidewalk, likely headed towards dinner.

"Those voices," he said.

Brenda paused for a moment. Waiting. He hadn't mentioned voices the last time he was here. What in the world was going on?

He looked at her, then down at the books in his arms, and then across the shop floor.

"What about the voices?" Brenda asked. "And what's your name?" She needed to tread carefully here, but she also needed to know what the boy's experience was and whether or not he knew anything.

"Lawrence," he said. "And I need help. They're not going away, no matter what I do. I wanted the Palo Santo for cleansing. As a matter of fact, the voices seem to be getting worse. And they're sounding kind of crazy."

"Crazy how? And my name's Brenda, by the way."

"Crazy like...like they're telling me to kill myself. They're telling me I should be ashamed of myself. I should be punished. Those sorts of things."

"Goddess, that sounds terrible. I'm so sorry you're going through this." Looking at the young man's aura, Brenda wouldn't think he would be hearing things like that. Not that you ever knew what was going on inside of people, but Lawrence seemed clear. Clean. Stable.

"Thing is, though, I feel like these voices aren't meant for me. Like they're not mine. You know what I mean?"

Brenda slid a Lon Milo DuQuette book onto the Kabbalah shelf, just past Rabbi David Cooper.

"You mean, as if someone else is sending them to you?" That sounded strange. Sendings like that were not unheard of, but not usual, either.

"Yeah, it's like...like someone's trying to drive me crazy. I mean, I've never felt like I wanted to kill myself. Sure, I'm upset or disappointed sometimes. Even pissed off at myself. But this?" He knelt down and pushed two books aside to insert another into its rightful place. The violin crescendoed, then fell silent for a moment, before new tune began.

"Let's sit for a while," Brenda said. There were only a few books left to shelve anyway, and Brenda needed to concentrate. Lawrence sat across from her and waited, hands on his thighs. She could smell damp denim and the sage Tempest had burned earlier in the day.

"I'm going to tell you something that might sound a little strange," Brenda said.

Lawrence smiled and shook his head. "You mean, like I didn't already come in here spouting some strange stuff?"

"Point taken. You're not the only one who's coming here, saying that voices are telling them strange things. People have been having dreams lately. Disturbing dreams. And voices accusing them of all sorts of things."

"You mean, you think someone's doing something to more than just me?"

"I have no idea yet," Brenda said. "All I know is that it's

starting to look an awful lot like a pattern. And I aim to get to the bottom of it."

Lawrence stood, picked up another book, looked at the cover, slid it into place on the ceremonial magic shelf.

"Can you teach me?" he said, his back to her, his shoulders very still. She knew it was an important question. She could feel his emotions, longing, hopeful, waiting.

"Teach you what?" He had to ask. He had to be specific.

He turned back toward her. "Teach me how to protect myself. Teach me how to do what you do. I want to learn. I've gotta protect my mind."

He sat back down again and leaned towards her, eyes intent. "You see, I got stuff I want to do with my life. Life is hard enough right now without someone sending voices into my head, telling me to kill myself. I want them gone. Can you help me?"

There it was again, that flickering inside of him. His magic. Brenda felt something like it every time someone came to her who was meant to be her student, her apprentice. She thought the coven was enough, that she wouldn't have to train anyone for a while

She guessed the Goddess had other ideas.

Okay Diana, she said. *Orders received.*

"If I take you on, it'll be a lot of work. You'll have to meditate every day, you'll have to learn to still your mind. You'll have to do a lot of things before we even get to some of the protections you're going to want or need. But meantime, if you agree, I'll give you some things to do to quiet the voices down."

Lawrence looked relieved. "Thank you."

"But I'll tell you one thing: along with learning to protect your mind, you're going to have to learn to be careful with that heart of yours."

He looked puzzled and tilted his head to the side. "What you mean?"

"You're an empath," Brenda said. "And you are telegraphing all over the place."

Brenda heard her phone ringing from the office. Damn. She stood again.

"Okay then," Lawrence said. "What do I have to do?"

"First thing is to take that Palo Santo you refused when you are in here the other day. Burn it around your bedroom to clear the space, and then draw a circle with it around your bed. Then before you go to sleep, and when you wake up in the morning, I want you to learn to count your breath. That's the first step toward calming your mind."

"I'll do whatever you need."

She knew she had to get to the phone. It had already stopped ringing, but it had *pinged* inside her aura. She didn't have time to start this young man's training right now.

She looked down at the table, at the one remaining book. It was a book on basic magical practice, and it would do.

Picking it up, she handed it to him. "Start with this. And come back in tomorrow."

A vision filled her head. She knew what to do then, about tracking down the source of the voices, but didn't want to. *I can't put him at risk!* she argued.

:*Give him the choice and his own destiny will unfold.*:
Damn it.

The young man was putting his jacket back on, tugging at the sleeves.

"Lawrence?"

He paused. "Yeah?"

"Would you be willing to be a guinea pig? Magically?"

"Whoa," he said, then fell silent. Brenda didn't say anything more. His choice.

"You gonna give me any more information than that?"

Relief filled her. She could read the energy around him. Courage. And acceptance. If he was needed, he would help.

:Guardian.:

"You're a guardian, did you know that?"

He shook his head. "I don't know what you're talking about."

"I think you do. But it's okay if you don't want to admit it yet. But you've got that spirit about you. And my idea is only half-formed at this point, but if you are willing, I *think* you can act as a goad, or a lure, to whomever or whatever is haunting all these people."

He sat back down, heavily, onto one of the chairs. "You mean, all this shit is really real?"

She didn't answer, just sat down herself again. She really needed to see who had called her, but this was more important.

"Ever since I was a kid, I wanted to believe. So yeah, if you'll agree to train me, I'll do whatever you need, as long as you promise me I'll be safe."

Brenda shook her head, sadly. "When it comes to magic, we can never promise anyone safety, Lawrence, but I *can* promise that my coven and I will do our utmost best to keep you as safe as we can."

He shrugged. "Makes sense to me. What do I gotta do?"

"Tell you what, let me talk with my coven, to see if my idea even has any merit, and then I'll call you. Okay?"

He held out his right hand. They shook.

"Okay."

26

CAROLINE

Caroline pulled the door open and pushed her way past a heavy velvet curtain. Very nice. The Ruby Lounge was beautiful. Red-and-amber glass lampshades cast warm pools of light down the long, narrow room, spilling across dark wooden benches and floors. Murals painted on wood panels lined each wall, one of fish swimming in an elaborate pond, the other, cranes flying over hills. The paintings framed the smiling faces of people out enjoying a quick meal or drink.

Under the murals, each wall had a long bench with small, two top tables in a row, each with a padded wooden chair on the other side. Some of the tables were shoved together for larger parties.

The bar itself was a curl of walnut near the back of the room, near low leather couches arranged in small groupings.

She didn't recognize the music playing—something with a heavy bass, vocals, and electronics—but unlike in some bars and restaurants, it was turned low enough that people could hear each other's conversations. Feeling a touch on her shoulder, she turned.

"Caroline," Brenda said, eyes sweeping over her face. She smelled of tuber roses and cold air. A new perfume.

"Brenda," Caroline replied. She found that she was smiling. Her joy at seeing Brenda standing there eclipsed the pain and trauma of the past few days. "Thanks for coming out on such short notice. I needed to talk with someone, and Sydney and Dan have had enough weirdness to deal with from me already. I figured they could use a night off."

Brenda gave her a quick hug, brushing a kiss lightly across her lips. It was too quick. Caroline pulled her in again, deepening the kiss. She felt Brenda relax, lips softening, before Caroline let go again.

"I'm glad you called," Brenda said, as a host approached them, menus in hand.

"Table for two?" he asked. "Or would you rather sit at the bar?"

"A table would be nice," Brenda replied.

Once they were settled, coats off, and drinks ordered, food menus in hand, Brenda turned her gaze on Caroline again. A small fluttering started up in Caroline's stomach. Attraction. Lust. Maybe even the early stirrings of love.

Had she ever felt this way with Rafe? She couldn't recall.

Brenda set down her menu just as the server, a petite Black woman with her hair in box braids, returned with their drinks. A martini for Caroline and a glass of Pinot Noir for Brenda. They placed their food orders and then Brenda raised her glass for a toast.

"To all the gifts of life."

Caroline gave a harsh laugh at that, but clinked her glass anyway. "To life."

The martini was good, with just a little bit of a bite. Caroline needed to calm down. Despite Brenda's soothing presence, she still felt rattled by what it happened at the support group. In the space of a week, she'd gone from feeling strong —free, even—to terrified, then hopeful, then freaked out. It was an ongoing, neverending loop. A spiral of emotions.

Brenda looked at her over the edge of her wine glass, light glinting off her jewelry and those all-knowing eyes that saw way too much.

That's what you get for hanging around with psychics, Caroline thought.

A tendril of dark hair brushed past Brenda's cheek and fell gently to her collarbone. The moonstone around her neck winked in the light of the votive candle in the center of their table. Caroline was stalling. She took another drink of her Sapphire martini. *Sapphire martini in the Ruby Lounge,* she thought. Yeah, definitely stalling.

A small crease appeared between Brenda's eyebrows. "Caroline, you sounded pretty desperate when you called, and not just for a date with me. Not that I don't appreciate sitting here staring at your lovely face, but I think you needed to talk about something. Isn't that right?"

Caroline sighed and set down her martini glass. She toyed with the long toothpick sticking through two fat green olives and what looked like pickled okra.

"You're right. Though I also wanted a date with you. It's really good to see you." She gave Brenda a small smile, then exhaled in a sigh. "I went to that support group meeting this afternoon."

"Oh? How was it?"

"I left before it started. There was a woman there.... Her name was Sharon. She was kind of crazy, although I'm not sure whether it was actual mental illness or..."

How in the world was she supposed to talk about this?

"Not sure whether it was actual mental illness, or what?"

"She said she'd been doing some sort of strange magic. Trying to get revenge. She wanted me to join her."

The server set a small dish of almonds down on the table. Caroline shoved a few of the nuts in her mouth. They were roasted with salt and rosemary.

"Did she say what sort of magic?"

Now it was Caroline's turn to furrow her brow. She shook her head. "I'm not sure. But it seemed as though she was trying to...I don't know, this sounds so strange."

Brenda took a sip of wine. And waited. She was so patient. It was one thing that struck Caroline about her. Caroline was not patient.

"I swear, she said she was trying to plant voices in people's heads."

Brenda knocked over her wine glass. A red cascade flowed across the table. Caroline jumped up. Both women grabbed their napkins and tried to stem the tide. The glass rolled, and Brenda caught it right before it fell off the edge of the table onto the floor.

Their server hurried over with a damp rag.

"I'm so sorry," Brenda said.

"That's okay," the woman said. "It happens all the time. Just let me clean this up, and I'll get you a fresh glass, all right?"

"Thank you so much."

When the waitress went to replace the glass of wine, the two women just stared at one another. Caroline knew something had just happened, but she wasn't sure what.

"Well, that was embarrassing," Brenda said, reaching for some almonds. She chewed for a moment, licked her lips, and finally spoke again. "I've had person after person come into my shop this last week...all of them hearing voices."

No wonder she had knocked over the wine glass.

"What kind of people?"

"All kinds. A few of them are just my usual customers...."

Caroline held very still, barely breathing. This was deeply, deeply strange. She clutched the medal of the Archangel Michael, hand fisted over her breastbone. Waiting.

"But some of those people?" Brenda grimaced and rubbed at her forehead. "They've been from the local government."

"Holy shit, are you serious?"

Brenda nodded. The waitress set down a fresh glass of Pinot Noir. Brenda thanked her profusely.

"Anything else I can get you?" the woman asked.

"No. Thanks so much."

Brenda sipped her wine until the server walked away.

"You said this was the support group for...?"

"For survivors of domestic violence and sexual abuse."

Brenda looked pale, too pale. Then her face flushed with what looked like anger.

"What are you thinking?" Caroline asked.

"I'm wondering if these political people aren't covering something up. Something to do with domestic violence. Or rape."

"And you think this woman, Sharon, is getting her revenge on them?"

Brenda shook her head, then leaned forward, voice low. "I don't know what to think. All I'm sure of is that up until four months ago, I pretty much took city government for granted. But after what the coven has seen. The corruption...I hate to say it, but very little surprises me anymore."

Caroline took a long drink of her martini and coughed. It burned a little going down. She appreciated the sensation. It reminded her that she was alive.

"I don't think I've thanked you enough. You and the coven." Tears filled Caroline's eyes. "I think you all saved my life."

"I think *he* did," Brenda said, pointing to her medal. "The Archangel." She nodded. "Now we just have to figure out what these other voices are and whether this woman you spoke to tonight is delusional, or actually has something to do with this."

Caroline nodded. She realized what a sheltered life she led so far. First raised in her upper-middle-class neighborhood, going to good schools, doing all the right activities. And then being more and more sequestered, isolated, by Rafe. Some of the literature Sydney had given her said that was pretty typical of abusers. They isolated their victims as a form of control.

But here she was now, drinking a martini in a dim lounge, across from a beautiful woman. A witch. And possibly saved by an archangel and a coven, and possibly hot on the heels of what? A delusional person? Or a powerful psychic sowing discord throughout the city?

"So you think this woman might be having an effect?"

"It all depends. It depends on whether or not she's had any training, or whether she's a natural psychic. Or whether, in her grief or rage or whatever it is, she didn't open up a channel strong enough to broadcast."

"I guess I have a lot to learn," Caroline said.

Brenda looked thoughtful, staring over Caroline's shoulder.

"Caroline?" Brenda caught her gaze. "What did the woman tonight look like?"

Caroline drew her image up. "Slightly older than we are. Maybe fifty? Blond, curly hair. A lot of it. Curvy, I think, though it was hard to tell. She was wearing this sort of sweater coat thing."

"Well damn."

"What?"

"I think I caught her stealing in the store this week. I had to ask her to leave."

27

BRENDA

Brenda rang the doorbell next to the glass door set between two bay windows. Traffic raced by behind her. The busy street seemed like a strange place for a temple, but she also knew folks rented what they could, where they could, if their group was too large to meet in someone's home.

Red curtains hung in the windows, obscuring what was inside. There was a banner in one of the windows, also red, with the elongated oval of the vesica piscis emblazoned on the fabric. Within the oval was a triangle with an eye in the center, a white dove flying downward, and a flaming chalice. White letters above and below the symbols read, "Light Eternal Lodge, Ordo Templi Orientis." The Thelemic Temple, they often called themselves, *thelema* being an ancient Greek word that represented the marriage of love and a person's will.

They were ceremonialists, and ceremonial magicians had different tools and techniques than witches, and she was really hoping Frater Louis could help her out.

The door opened on a smiling man with dark salt-and-pepper hair, dressed in all black.

"Brenda! Welcome! I was so happy to hear from you," Frater Louis said. "It's been entirely too long."

"Thanks for making the time to see me, I know you're busy." Brenda looked around. She hadn't been in the local Thelemic Temple in years. The front room Louis ushered her into wasn't the sanctuary itself, of course. The ritual space was behind a set of double doors to the back. This front area was just a meeting hall where they held lectures, study groups, and the occasional party. It was a comfortable enough place. Nice, actually.

The wood floors were strewn with warming rugs in jewel tones; the walls, lined with bookcases and devotional art. A small kitchen area was set up on a cabinet near a single door that Brenda recalled led to the toilets.

Padded wooden folding chairs were arrayed in stacks along the back wall opposite the doors. Years of incense permeated the rugs, books, and walls. For the first time, Brenda wondered what sensitive people did about joining magical groups. She couldn't imagine how they managed without migraines.

Frater Louis led her to a study table surrounded by five chairs. An older Latino man, he'd been part of the OTO since the 1960s. Brenda liked and respected Louis. He carried himself with a natural sense of authority, shoulders straight and spine erect. His brown skin was slightly pock-marked, but Brenda barely noticed, his face was that beautiful. Dark brown eyes, a Roman nose, and full, dark lips. But mostly? His beauty came from the energy he radiated.

Louis was a self-possessed magician, and to Brenda, that was one of the most attractive things in the world. If she'd been into men, she would have approached Louis years ago.

He waved Brenda into a chair. "Please, sit. Can I get you some sparkling water? Coffee?"

Brenda shook her head. "No thanks. I'd rather just get down to business."

Frater Louis sat across from Brenda and folded his hands together on top of the table. She glanced at his thick silver ring. Another dove, set in the vesica pisces.

"So, what can I do for you?"

Brenda closed her eyes for a moment and took in a deep breath. She asked her spirit guides for help. She also called upon the Voice. Might as well use it, if it was going to keep intruding on her life.

She dropped her attention deep inside herself, down into her center. *Give me the correct information*, she thought. *Let me ask the right questions, and hear the right answers. Please.*

"Well, I'm not sure whether I'm dealing with angels or demons, or both. All I know is I'm hearing a voice, and a lot of my customers have been hearing voices, too. And then...a new friend of mine encountered someone who said she'd been seeding people's thoughts. Tangentially, I also caught the same woman stealing from the Inner Eye."

Frater Louis just raised one hand as if to say go on. He was almost preternaturally self-contained. She looked past his shoulder, eyes scanning the bookcases, but not seeing the titles on the spines. Buying time to search her thoughts.

"I'm not sure if these visitations are connected. But I'm also not sure that they aren't. And some of them seem benign, actually, even helpful. The voices I've been hearing" —she paused a moment, then corrected herself—"the *Voice* I've been hearing, well, my coven is pretty convinced it's an angel. It arrives on a shaft of light. Also, my new friend? The Archangel Michael seems to be an ally of hers. He burned the shit out of the hands of a man who was trying to hurt her."

Frater Louis leaned forward, hands clasped again, arms sliding across the table toward her. If the table hadn't been so large, he could have reached out and touched her at this point.

"A physical manifestation? How?"

"Through a sacred medal. He grabbed it, and the image burned him."

He stroked his chin. "Impressive. And the other voices?"

"They're frightening people. They're scaring a wide variety of people, from ordinary students and waitresses, all the way up to..." She paused, not sure if she should say anymore. She took her priestess's vows pretty seriously, and didn't want to disclose too much. But she also needed help.

Frater Louis caught her discomfort, and slid his hands away, sitting upright once again.

"I can, and will, hold all this in confidence," he said.

Brenda nodded, and puffed out a breath.

"This goes all the way up to judges, and the chief of police. Maybe even beyond that, but those are just the people who have come to me so far."

He expelled a heavy breath. "No shit," he said, then tapped a finger on his lips. Thinking.

"How much do you know about the seventy-two bright spirits?" he asked.

Brenda shrugged. She'd heard of them, of course. She couldn't run a metaphysical shop and not have.

"It's not something I've studied in depth. I'm a witch. We don't usually work with those sorts of forces. But I know that they are considered to be angelic entities, right? That's what you all do with the angelic languages, and Enochian magic...."

Frater Louis was nodding.

"That's true. All of that is true. We do work with the angels in that way, and there are traditionally said to be seventy-two of them." He shrugged and smiled. "But of course, these things can't be measured, can they?"

Brenda traced a finger across the wooden table, following the grain up to the tangled dark whorls of a knot. "I suppose not. 'There are more things in heaven and earth' and all that, right?"

"'Than are dreamt of in your philosophy'," he finished the Shakespeare quote. "The thing is, there's also the flip side. Goetia."

"Demons," Brenda said.

"That's right. And you know that some of us in the OTO work with the demons as helpers. We form a compact, an agreement. They do the work we need, and then we work to lift them up to a higher, more sublime plane. Closer to the angels."

"To redeem them," Brenda said.

"To redeem them, and redeem ourselves. Some people are agnostic, and posit that angels and demons are both just parts of ourselves that we need to deal with. Others work with them as discrete entities."

Something itched at her skin. Brenda felt restless all of a sudden, finding it hard to sit, having a calm conversation about these things. Not when she didn't know whether or not people were in danger.

"So what are you saying?" she asked.

"What I'm saying is, a lot of us have a theory... Some of us even have the experience." And he paused, and placed both hands flat on the table. Then he looked at her as if to make sure she was truly listening.

"I'm ready."

"Many of us suspect that the beings we call angels and the beings we call demons, whether they exist inside, outside, or somewhere in between, are simply reflections of each other."

"And?"

"I'm saying that often we *name* things demons or angels, because of how we perceive them acting in our lives, but really we're talking about the same thing."

"And what's that?"

"Forces too powerful for the human mind to understand without cracking into bits."

Well, damn again.

Frater Louis steepled his hands beneath his chin, dark eyes flashing.

"So, are there seventy-two of each, or do we just badly perceive what we see in the mirror?" he asked.

"How do we tell the difference?"

"Does it matter? In working any sort of magic, and in dealing with any forces, whether internal or external, we must know *ourselves* to the best of our abilities. We look at the world from there, and the cleaner our internal processes are, the clearer the reflection in all the worlds. We do what we can in order to act with confidence, and without fear."

"I know all this, but...I think I just got shaken."

"I do sense an angelic presence around you, by the way."

How much more confirmation do you need, Brenda? Stop fighting this.

"What's the first thing an angel traditionally says when they appear to a human?"

"Be not afraid."

"There's a reason for that," he said. "They know they're going to freak you out, for one thing, but they also know that in order to face the challenge they bring to your doorstep, you're going to need to step up. Getting past fear is the first thing you need to deal with."

"It's either getting past the fear or learning how to act with courage regardless."

"Exactly." he said, "It strikes me that what you need to do is remember what your will is. What is your primary motivation? What threads through your entire life?"

Brenda thought for a moment.

"To teach. To serve the light the Sun and the Moon— in the form of Lucifer and Diana," she said. "To serve the people to the best of my ability. But mostly?"

Brenda paused. A truth she didn't often seek out stirred inside her.

:Bring forth that which is slumbering in darkness. Know thyself,: the Voice said.

What was it? What was her truth? Her task? Her will?

"Mostly—and I don't know why I didn't figure this out until now—mostly my will is to work for the liberation of all beings."

"And *that* is why you work with the deities you do. They are all about light and liberation, despite what popular culture might say. You were marked, likely years ago, as one whom the people could trust. And your Gods have worked through you."

Brenda wished she'd accepted that cup of tea now. She could use it.

"It is also likely the reason these angels are coming to you. And the reason all of these people are appearing, too."

"Angels plural?"

He looked startled. "Yes. You've named Michael and Lucifer both in the course of this conversation."

"Oh Goddess. How have I been so stupid? Since I work

with Lucifer as Diana's brother, the sun to her moon, I always forget he's also a Goddamned angel!"

Frater Louis laughed. "Only damned according to one of the stories."

"So what do I do now?" she asked.

"*We*," he corrected, "are going to make some tea, and talk some more about how angels and demons work in the world."

"And then?"

"We're going to figure out whether or not we need to stop them, or offer them our aid."

28

CAROLINE

Still a bit worn out from the physical altercation, and then from all the information swirling in her head, Caroline decided to go for a drive.

The coven had dealt with Rafe. She couldn't do anything about that woman, Sharon, and whatever the heck she may or may not have been doing to poison the Portland airwaves with psychic interference. Whatever that was. Not being a trained psychic or a witch, she couldn't help Brenda with the people hearing voices, either.

But she could do something about her business.

If she was going to build a new life, or even have a chance at it, she needed to make some changes.

She had invoked freedom the other evening. Freedom and love. Well, she had two sample cases filled with gemstones and jewelry that might go a long way toward helping with the first.

She just had to take some action.

Over a cup of tea in Dan and Sydney's kitchen that morning, Caroline realized she'd already made begun the first change that might boost sales and help grow her business. She could visit more shops, talk with the proprietors, and ask them what they wanted in person.

"Nothing like the personal touch," she said she pulled into a parking spot in downtown Salem, Oregon.

It was a lovely day. The storm had broken, leaving behind ragged white clouds that swept across the blue sky. Blooming cherry trees lined the streets, showing off pink and white and deep rose petals cascading softly to the sidewalks. She took in a deep breath of the fresh air, and locked the Jeep.

Downtown Salem was cute. Brick-fronted buildings with bright awnings were interspersed with plaster-fronted buildings that looked like they had been built in the 1920s. Caroline found the red brick charming. That was something they didn't have much of down in earthquake central. Wood and steel were the building materials of the San Francisco Bay Area.

She had purposefully parked several blocks away from her target, Witch's Brew, so she could explore a little. She left her sample case in the car for now, figuring she'd scope things out first. As far as she could tell, Witch's Brew was a combination coffee and tea house and magic shop. She looked forward to seeing how it worked.

Salem was quieter than Portland, but the state capital was busy enough for a weekday. People wandered in and out of the shops, businesses, and restaurants that lined the street.

Zipping up the new quilted blue coat she'd bought the day Rafe had abducted her, she slung her purse across her body and tucked her hands into her pockets. She was determined to enjoy the day.

Walking underneath the cherry trees, Caroline lingered at shop windows, peering in at bright, blue-and-ochre woven scarves and textured jackets. Another store was filled with walking boots and shoes. A shop with kitschy house-wares flanked a bookstore. Maybe she would stop by there before she left for home. Get Dan a gift for feeding her so well.

Funny that. She was already thinking of Portland as home. Sydney and Dan had been just great. They told her she could stay as long as she needed to. She had a feeling she'd be finding a place of her own within a month or two, but it was nice not to feel rushed. To have room to figure out some things about her life.

About how she planned to move forward.

Maybe she'd stop in the bookstore, she mused, and pick up some science fiction, or a romance. She'd loved romance in high school, especially historicals, but Rafe had sneered at them, and she'd stopped reading the books rather than deal with his scorn.

She batted at the back of her head. It felt like some sort of insect was buzzing near her neck.

"I guess that's one of the perils of spring," she said. "Bugs."

Her back began to itch, first down low, near her spine. As she reached around to scratch, it moved up between her shoulder blades.

"Damn it." She couldn't quite reach. She'd just have to hope it went away on its own. Tucking her hands back into her coat pockets, she walked on, trying to ignore the itch.

Witch's Brew was right across the street, with a stylized swoop of black giving the hint of the curve of a black cat wearing a traditional peaked witch's hat painted on the awning. She waited for the light to change. The itching wasn't going away. If anything, it was growing stronger.

Caroline hoped it wasn't a recurrence of the eczema

she'd had a few years before. The doctor said the skin condition was exacerbated by stress, and she'd certainly had enough of that the past week.

The light changed. She started across the street when a voice behind her called her name.

"Caroline!"

Oh no. Not *that* voice. Not him. The itching and tingling increased, along with a sense that she was being tugged backward. What the hell was going on?

And how in the world had Rafe found her?

Once she got to the opposite sidewalk, she turned, slowly, then backed up toward Witch's Brew, trying to get as much sidewalk between her and him as possible. She also wanted to be near the door to the shop, in case she needed backup.

It wouldn't be a good first impression on her clients, but all Caroline cared about right now was staying safe.

Rafe looked like hell. His usually perfect dark hair was uncombed, his jacket had a rip at the collar, and there was a bruise high up on his left cheek. Looking down, she saw that loose white bandages wrapped both hands.

She couldn't feel badly about that. Heart thumping faster, she planted her feet more firmly on the sidewalk and took her hands out of her pockets.

"Stay back," she said.

He slowed his walk, then stepped up on the sidewalk, face darkening with rage. She peered into his eyes. Even at the slight distance, she could see that beyond the rage, there was bewilderment. His little toy had just woken up, and he was discovering it could bite.

"Why did you do that?" he asked.

What the hell was he talking about?

"I'm not the one who did something, Rafe. That's all on you."

He took two more steps toward her. She held up both her hands. He stopped again.

He was too close for her to feel comfortable. Maybe backing up against the storefront had been a bad idea. There was nowhere else for her to go now.

Rafe darted his head from side to side, then licked his lips. Then, seeming to settle on something, he turned his face back towards her, the rictus of a smile cracking his lower face. As if she would be fooled by that.

"Come on, baby," he said. His voice was soft, just loud enough to carry over the midday traffic and the conversations of the people walking by.

A woman slowed her walk, and raised a questioning eyebrow Caroline's way. Caroline smiled and shook her head. No way did she want to involve someone in this. Not if she didn't have to. The woman walked on.

That's an old habit, isn't it? Keeping other people safe. The thought flashed across her mind, so quick it was barely a blip.

"I want you to come back with me," Rafe was saying. "Come back home. We can go to counseling if you want. I know you're upset, and I don't blame you. Shouldn't have made you come with me like that. But I'm willing to do what it takes to get you back."

"I'm not coming back, Rafe."

The smile shifted to a sneer as his lips compressed. The flush returned, creeping up his neck and staining his face red.

In that moment, he looked so ugly, Caroline couldn't imagine how she'd ever found him attractive. How he'd ever charmed her.

Rafe moved again, two steps forward. The itching along her back increased, and the medal at her breastbone warmed and hummed. It felt as if the amethyst point jumped in response.

"Stop!" Every alarm inside her was sounding, so loud inside her head it was practically deafening.

Then he closed the distance between them and shot out a bandaged hand.

And then, all of a sudden, he was there. The Archangel. Michael. Standing between her and Rafe, a shimmering shaft of light. She could barely see him through the brilliance, but she felt it when Rafe stopped.

And she could see that the angel carried a sword.

The shop door opened next to her. A woman's voice, speaking. "Are you okay? Is he trying to hurt you?"

"Take me inside. Please."

"Yes."

Warm hands on her arms, warm brown eyes set in deep brown skin, a worried crease between thick, arched brows.

And then, they were inside. In a place that smelled of coffee, and cinnamon, chocolate, and cardamom. And peace. It smelled like peace.

"Thank you so much," Caroline said to her rescuer as the woman led her to a small round café table with a marble top and dark wood legs. The woman pulled out a stuffed dining chair and gently pushed Caroline down.

Another woman, this one with skin pale as the white cherry blossoms outside, blond stubble haloing her head, came over with a pot of tea and a blue china cup.

"Aztec chocolate," she said. "It'll be good for the shock."

"Thanks, Lindy," the first woman said.

Caroline realized she was shaking. She looked out the

window. She couldn't see Rafe anymore, but the shimmering light was still there.

Michael? She flung her purse off her back and unzipped her coat. She needed to get to the medal.

"I'm sorry. I just..." Once her fingers closed around the metal, and the amethyst was once again resting just beneath the heel of her hand, she felt better. Like she could calm down.

The Black woman sat across from her. She smelled of sandalwood and amber. A woven purple scarf, like the ones Caroline had seen in the shop window down the street, coiled around her head, clearly holding in a mass of hair.

"That your boyfriend? Husband? Do we need to call the cops? Or someone to come get you?"

"I think... No."

"Drink your chocolate." The woman poured some of the steaming brew into the delicate blue cup and set it in front of Caroline. "Go ahead."

Caroline took a tentative sip. It was delicious. Chocolate, cinnamon, and the bite of cayenne. She drank some more. The woman was right, it helped.

"It's my husband, but I'm trying to get away. I thought... he'd been taken care of. I have no idea how he even found me."

The woman looked *around* the edges of Caroline's body, in that way Brenda and Raquel had, as though she was seeing something ordinary eyes couldn't catch.

The woman nodded.

"That dude's corded into you.... It's weird. The cords are braided so tightly, at first I mistook them for your own energy signature. It's a wonder you got away at all. Some strong magic must be helping you. My name's Shani, by the way."

"Caroline." Caroline took another sip of chocolate. Her brain finally stopped stuttering and kicked in. "So, cords? I assume you mean some sort of energetic tie. And...what do you suggest I do about them?"

"With your permission, I can help you cut them, calling your energy back to you, and sending your stalker husband on his way."

29

BRENDA

"I can't believe he came after you! We disabled his tracking systems and I *know* Selene's binding was effective." Brenda and Caroline talked as quietly as they could over the music piping through the big yuppie food store down the street from the Inner Eye. Sly and the Family Stone. Too bad Brenda was unable to enjoy it.

She had no desire to be shopping, but if the coven was going to do ritual to stop whatever the heck was going on in Portland, they were going to need food. And afterward? They might even want some wine. Funny, the coven had never done more than drink the occasional glass, but since the events of the past few months?

Well, they still didn't drink before magic or ritual, so as not to mess up the workings, but after? For some of Arrow and Crescent, the single glass had turned into two or three. She and Raquel were going to need to keep an eye on that. Make sure magical discipline didn't break down and no one's health became compromised.

Brenda pushed the small, double basket cart past the deli, before pausing to look over the cheese display.

"Well, he couldn't get at me," Caroline replied, "so the binding worked that way. And he looked terrible, as though something was eating away at him. The witch I met, Shani, said Rafe found me through some energy cords. She helped me cut them."

Brenda stopped the basket. "Cords. Damn it. I have no idea how we missed those. Rookie mistake."

"Shani said they were so tightly wound, they almost looked like my own energy."

"We still should have seen them. Shani has a good reputation. I'm glad she could help you." Brenda wheeled the cart forward again, before pausing to consider the relative merits of manchego and Havarti. She tossed both into the cart.

"How do you feel now?" Brenda perused the bins of olives beneath the sneeze guard, and began packing a plastic tub with large green Spanish olives.

"I feel better. More free. But I felt that way after you all got me away from him, too. So I don't know if I can trust that. And it still bugs me that he chased me down to Salem. Makes me wonder if I shouldn't go to the cops after all."

When Caroline looked at Brenda, Brenda wanted nothing more than to kiss her, right there in the middle of the grocery aisle.

"Do you want to?"

Caroline shook her head no, the shining sheet of black hair drifting across her narrow shoulders.

"You have backup now. You aren't alone," Brenda said. Instead of pulling Caroline toward her, she pushed the cart down the cracker aisle, which was immediately blocked by another shopping cart. Brenda sighed. She'd hoped that by hitting the store before the after-work rush, they would have avoided traffic jams in the aisles.

"You're that psychic woman!"

A woman with curly blond hair leaned over her cart. Oh. Just great. It was her shoplifter. And apparently, it was also the woman Caroline had met at the support group. Sharon.

"You tried to keep me from getting the tools I needed to do my work!" Her eyes looked wild, and energy swirled around her body. The woman was completely ungrounded.

"I believe what happened was that I stopped you from stealing from my shop," Brenda replied.

The woman banged her cart into Brenda's. Caroline stepped forward, holding out one hand.

"Sharon. Stop. Whatever you think you're doing, Brenda isn't harming you."

Sharon whipped her head toward Caroline. "You. I thought you might help me, but you're just like everyone else. No one cares about my daughter. Not the police. Not the judges. Not her." She pointed straight at Brenda.

Police? Judges? Maybe she *was* haunting people. But that didn't explain the others who were also hearing voices.

"Women are in danger," Sharon said, more quietly this time. She picked absently at a piece of loose skin on her lips. "You are interfering with justice. There are demons in the government, and you don't even care! My daughter went to the police for help after her assault, and what did they do? They raped her! Then laughed at her. And that judge? Another *woman*! Did nothing. *Nothing!*"

Oh, sweet Goddess. The police *raped this woman's daughter?* Brenda made sure she was centered, and sent soothing energy out through her aura. *Diana, be with me. Lend me your certainty and strength.*

"Sharon?" she said, as calmly and quietly as she could, "do you want to talk about this? To see if there's any way we can help you?"

The woman gripped the handle of her shopping cart, her knuckles showing red. The blond corkscrews of her hair obscured her face for a moment. Brenda thought she heard her sigh. She felt Caroline beside her, breathing softly. Sly and the Family Stone segued into a second song. It all felt so surreal, standing in the middle of the grocery aisle, with a woman babbling about voices, and revenge.

A shopping cart entered the other end of the aisle before the old man pushing it looked, frowned, and backed away, shaking his head.

Good choice, Brenda thought.

Sharon's head snapped up. "You. You have an angel around you." She looked toward Caroline. "You, too. Both of you. Angels. Angels of light. Avengers. Avenging angels."

"Sharon, how can we help you?"

Sharon held on to her cart, backing it away. "Use your angels. Use your angels to help avenge. Seed the voices. You have to help me. You have to help me seed the voices. If they won't bring me justice, we bring justice to them. Understand? Understand? *Do you?*"

Sharon's voice escalated, becoming louder and louder with every utterance.

Brenda opened her heart to all the woman's pain, all the anguish, the rending, the tearing of heart and soul until they were fragments, strips of flesh flayed off of bone. She didn't know how anyone could survive such a thing. No wonder the woman's mind had shattered.

"Something wrong here?" a male voice behind her asked.

Brenda didn't want to take her eyes off Sharon's face, she was afraid of what the woman might do. Luckily, she heard Caroline murmur, "She's just upset. We've both met her before, and are trying to help. We'll get her out of your way as soon as we can."

Oh no. Brenda prayed Sharon hadn't heard that.

"Out of the way? That's what *they* all said. They all wanted Sharon out of the way. Well, I'm showing them, aren't I? I'm showing up in their *dreams*."

She rammed her cart forward, smashing into Brenda's cart. Brenda wasn't prepared. The cart slammed into her belly and hips, and she stumbled backward, into Caroline.

Caroline fell. Brenda turned to see her friend on the floor, with the grocery clerk, a young man, trying to help her up. When she looked back at Sharon, the woman had abandoned her cart and was running away.

"Should I go after her?" Brenda asked. Caroline was upright by this time, brushing at her pants and wincing. She rubbed at her elbow, clearly in pain. Damn it. Following on what that bastard of her husband had done, that tumble must have hurt.

"Just leave her," Caroline said. "Just leave her be."

"Are you okay ma'am?" The clerk asked.

"I will be, thanks."

"Do you want to press charges?"

"Oh! No. No. I think her life is painful enough as it is."

Brenda agreed. Sharon was a disturbed psychic, the kind that all too often ended up on the streets or in prison, or trying to numb themselves with drugs, sugar, or alcohol.

A wash of sadness filled her. Damn it.

"Well, I guess I'll put these groceries away," the clerk said, disentangling the two carts.

Caroline looked at Brenda. "Do you have enough supplies yet?"

Brenda looked down at her cart. The last thing she wanted to do was finish shopping. And the last thing she wanted to do after that was have a meeting to decide how the hell the coven was going to deal with this mess that grew more complex and less straightforward by the minute.

Good job, angels, she thought. *I thought you guys were supposed to be helpful.*

Was Sharon possessed by something? Or had she just become a distorted mirror, twisting the face of justice into something her shattered mind could recognize?

There are forces too vast for the human mind to understand, Frater Louis had said. And whether that force was a demon, or the depth of human evil, it didn't matter, Brenda saw.

She just hoped her angels were enough to save Sharon, and to save the innocent people caught in the overflow of her madness.

The whole city was being poisoned, and, much as Brenda wanted justice, she couldn't allow Sharon to work her magic this way.

Hypocrite, her inner voices said. Maybe so. But a witch had to draw her boundaries somewhere. Right or wrong.

"I think crackers, cheese, and wine are going to have to do it. Let me pay for this and we can get out of here." Brenda pushed the cart toward the cashier's stands in the front of the store.

She just hoped what the coven was planning wasn't a mistake that would cost more than they were willing to pay.

30

CAROLINE

"Your coven says you're all about justice, but what does justice look like?" Caroline said.

The longer this discussion went on, the more angry she felt. Everything bubbled up inside of her: her rage at her husband, her rage at the injustice of what it sounded like Sharon's daughter, —and Sharon herself—had gone through.

And now, her rage at this group of people, who were supposed to be there to help.

They were meeting in Brenda's living room, which was a beautiful, soothing place. It had pale green walls, a riot of artwork depicting red, blue, gold, and green Goddesses and Gods. Over the fireplace mantle was a brilliant painting of the sun dancing with the moon.

She would've liked this place at any other time. But right now, Caroline refused to be soothed. She refused to be charmed. It was hard to even look at Brenda, this woman she was so drawn to. The woman she would like nothing more than to fall into bed with, spending hours getting to know each other's bodies. Making good on the promise of those few kisses they'd had time to share.

Caroline wanted that, so badly. But wanting didn't take away the sense of anger and betrayal she felt right now.

Raquel laid a hand on Caroline's arm. They were sitting on a forest-green couch, next to one another. Some of the other coven members sat in chairs, or perched on ottomans. A couple of people had dragged in chairs from the dining room. The room was filled with Brenda's coven, Joshua from The Road Home, and a neatly dressed man with salt-and-pepper hair and a pockmarked face. Caroline had never seen him before, Louis they called him. Something Louis. Some honorific she couldn't remember.

"Sometimes justice looks different than we want it to," Raquel said. Raquel smelled of coffee and mint. She was someone that Caroline could see liking. Trusting, even.

"What is that supposed to mean?"

"It means," Louis said, "that we humans can only comprehend one or two events at a time. Mostly simple things. Intelligent as we are, we're not smart enough. It's part of why we do magic, and train our minds. All of that increases our capacity to comprehend."

Caroline looked at Brenda. Her head was bowed, staring at her hands. Her dark brown hair framed her pale face. She looked almost defeated. Caroline wasn't sure if that was true, or if she was just thinking.

All Caroline knew right now was that the light around Brenda was as strong as ever. Funny, that woman, Sharon, said she saw an angel around Caroline, too. Years of being ground down and gaslighted by Rafe, made to feel as small as possible, and all of a sudden, she had two angels in her life.

Maybe they'd always been there. Rafe had never beaten her, just threatened to. Maybe the angels kept him in check. Caroline stroked her thumb across the Archangel Michael medal. She hoped he was there. But right now, she wasn't sure if he was doing any good.

Joshua was tucked into a corner near the fireplace, sitting on one of the end chairs from the dining room, legs crossed, arms resting on the wooden arms of the chair. He still looked as if he'd stepped out of a play, or some Gothic revue. He tapped his beringed fingers together and cleared his throat, as though he were about to speak.

"Caroline, I hate to say it, but I think Raquel and Frater Louis are correct. This is a very tangled situation, and as I see it, part of our job is to begin the untangling. To see what actual help we can offer, instead of just rushing in to try to fix things before we know what in the world were doing."

"Anyone else have anything to say?" Raquel asked. Caroline looked around the room. No one else moved to speak.

"I just don't see how you can't agree to help this woman. What happened to her daughter sounds egregious. And as far as I can tell, she's taking the law into her own hands. Frankly, it sounds like you all have done the same in the past, so why in the hell would you not help her? Why in the hell would you want to help some judge or the chief of police instead of *her*, a woman who was wronged by the very system you say you've been fighting?" She looked at Tobias and Moss in particular. And then at Cassiel.

Cassiel leaned forward, one of her long red curls falling over her shoulder. "We aren't trying to impede justice, Caroline. We're trying to get to some semblance of the truth. Sometimes that's the hardest job. I understand feeling angry, and I even think it's right. You think we are not all pissed off about what happened? You think we don't want justice?"

Finally, Brenda sat up, ramrod straight. The light around her pulsed and flared. She closed her eyes and opened them. Closed and opened them. It wasn't blinking. It was as though she was looking inward and then out again. Over and over. Or as if the angel around her wanted its say.

Her face looked ethereal. Luminous. As though she were lit from within.

"The messengers remind us that it is not just one soul that we must save. Our work here is the liberation of the city. And the well-being of its people. And the well-being of all the peoples on this earth. Every human, every animal, every insect, every tree and flower and drop of water, too. All of these need our attention. And we must call upon our allies and use our magic to right wrongs to the best of our ability. But it is our job to right the *deeper* wrongs."

Brenda stared straight at Caroline then, but looking from that beautiful face? Those were not Brenda's eyes. They were the eyes of an angel. Of some vast, dark, celestial being. Caroline could barely breathe. She clutched at the Michael medallion so hard, the image of the crossed sword and wing must have imprinted itself onto her thumb.

"The deeper wrongs shall not be made right by punishing those who should never be punished. Harmony shall never be restored by spreading sickness among the healthy. It is our job to seek restoration. To move from the five into the six. To move through battle toward true harmony. The song that every star must sing before it dies. Seeks to repair the wounds."

Brenda shut her eyes, and it felt as though every person in the room inhaled together.

"Well, that was cryptic," Lucy remarked.

"Protein," Brenda said. Caroline had no idea why until Moss grabbed some slices of cheese, put them on a napkin, and placed the napkin into Brenda's hands.

"Eat some cheese, Brenda. Once you get some protein in you, you can have a sip of wine." He paused in thought for a moment. "Unless the angel wants to speak some more. Then I'll get you some water."

"I'll get it," Lucy said, springing up from her place on the floor and heading into the kitchen.

Caroline still didn't know what all this meant. She was no less confused than she had been before. But at least some of her anger had dissipated

"So what we do?" she asked.

"My intuition tells me we have to work with that young man, Lawrence," Brenda said. "He came into the shop for a reason. Twice. He wants training, but he's also one of those who's been hearing the voices. He's willing to help if we need him."

"He's willing to be a conduit? Or a guinea pig?" That was Louis asking.

Brenda nodded, then bit off the end of another piece of cheese. Lucy came back in, and handed her a tumbler filled with water. Brenda drank down half the glass.

"Help me understand," Caroline said. "If what I'm hearing is correct, there are *two* injustices we're fighting. Or two illnesses, as the angel said. If that *was* an angel." She shook her head, half in disbelief, half just to lighten the mood for a moment.

"So how do we know how to approach this? How do we know which injustice to address?" Caroline turned to Brenda. She still looked surreal, so beautiful, it was difficult for Caroline to not reach out and cup her hands around her face, and just breathe in that beauty.

"So this is what it is to stare upon the face of a God," she murmured, forgetting what it was she'd been about to say.

"Not a God," Brenda said. "But not quite me either."

Then Brenda closed her eyes again, and sank back into her chair.

Caroline inhaled, exhaled, and shook out her hands, trying to remind herself that she was human in the midst of all the strange energy pulsing in the living room. She needed to remember that she had a body. The air felt so strange, but she breathed in anyway, and shifted her hand from the archangel medal to her amethyst point, seeking...words.

"Let me try again," she said. "We need to stop Sharon from harming innocent people. We need to protect the ones that have just gotten in her way. I get that much. But how do we do that, and still bring Sharon and her daughter some healing? How do we do that, and find some of what she's calling justice?"

Raquel set down her cup of tea and nodded. "Those are the questions we need to address. And whatever magic we're about to do over the next day or two—and it does need to be over the next day or two because things are getting worse—we're just gonna have to plan our best and hope. Hope that one or more of us gets enough insight into this that we can be of help."

She shifted so she was looking at Caroline again. "The thing about magic, is that it's always a risk." Raquel coiled a finger around one of her dreadlocks, then patted it back into place. "But we've all taken on the responsibility to shoulder that risk. Sometimes we don't *know*. But we always have to *try*."

Caroline took a sip of wine.

"Then I guess I'll try, too."

But damn, she wished this coven had more solid answers.

31

BRENDA

"So what do I gotta do?" Lawrence asked.

The Inner Eye wasn't open yet, and Raquel had Cassiel working the café. The coven had decided that getting the magical operation done sooner rather than later was important. And if Lawrence was going to come on board, they had to figure that out right away.

Which meant this morning.

So Brenda, Raquel, Lawrence, and Frater Louis all sat around the big wooden table in the back room of the Inner Eye, surrounded by the Elemental Banners. There was no music on yet, just the slight hum from the lights, and the trickle of the water fountain that sat next to the counter in the main room. And in the echo of Lawrence's question, hanging in the air.

Everyone had a mug of coffee or tea in front of them, and a plate of muffins, cheese Danish, and even a couple of gluten-free pastries sat in the center. Other than Lawrence, who happily munched on a corn muffin, no one was touching any of them.

Everyone else is too keyed up, Brenda thought. *We know how serious this is.*

She knew *she* was tense, despite doing a longer prayer and meditation session that morning. She blew across her mug of green tea, wishing it was coffee, but knowing that her stomach wouldn't take the acids anyway.

Raquel leaned forward, elbows on the table, hands clasped beneath her chin. She looked tired. Brenda figured *she* probably did too. She certainly felt it. Lawrence, being young, looked fresh as all get out. It was hardly fair.

Lawrence's T-shirt was red, with a *Star Trek* emblem on the left side of his chest. Brenda seemed to recall that was some sort of in-joke, but she hadn't watched the show enough to remember what exactly the reference was.

"It's a big experiment," Raquel said, "and frankly I have concerns about us even trying it with you. Not that you're not a nice young man, I'm sure you are. But I'd rather not have someone untested and untrained taking a risk like this."

"She's right, Lawrence," Brenda replied. She set down her mug but kept her hands wrapped around it, enjoying the warmth. "But if you're willing, it's frankly our best shot. And that's why you're getting a crash course in some basic techniques this morning. I'm just thankful you had the time."

Lawrence tapped his fingers on his coffee mug. He tilted his head to the side. "And still...neither of you has told me what exactly this ritual will entail. What are you going to want from me? How's it going to work?"

"Well," Raquel answered, "the reason I said it was a risk isn't just that *all* magic is risky—which it is—but it's that frankly, we don't know what the hell we're doing this time."

Frater Louis cleared his throat. He had sat, ramrod

straight in his chair, quietly drinking his coffee this whole time. But it seemed as if it was his time to speak now. Brenda hoped he had something useful to contribute, because she didn't. Her stomach was tied up in knots, she knew Caroline was upset, and frankly, she was a little bit afraid. The angel had gone quiet. *Bastard,* she thought. Just when she needed the Voice, the Voice wasn't there.

"Don't scare the young man," Louis said. "Lawrence, let me lay out for you what we think is going to happen. A large group of us discussed this long into the night, and yes, some of it we're going to have to play by ear. Think of it is freestyle jazz..."

"Okay?" Lawrence set down the muffin and picked up his coffee mug.

"This woman, Sharon, is linked to you somehow. And the thing I sense around you, and that Raquel and Brenda sense too, is that energetic cords connect you to this woman. We don't know how they attach to you. We don't know if you happened to be walking by her one day when she was broadcasting, or if you're just incredibly psychically sensitive."

"Frankly, I think that's what it is." Brenda said. "You have talent. It's part of what drew you here. I wouldn't doubt that the others caught in the crossfire are also sensitive."

Lawrence nodded, took a sip of coffee, and then placed both hands palm down on the table. "So..."

"So," Louis continued, "we try to trace the cords back to her, and then we try to see what other cords she's broadcasting outward and see if we can cut them off at the source."

"Ha," Lawrence said. "Sounds weird, but if it's going to help stop these damn voices in my head, asking me to kill myself, I'm all for it. I'm not going to investigate behind the big rock, either."

That was it. That was the joke of his T-shirt. Whoever wore the red shirt on *Star Trek* ended up dead. Brenda grinned at Lawrence. He grinned back. Laughing in the face of danger.

He picked up his muffin again, taking a large bite.

"All right then," Raquel said. "We need to get you ready. I want to take you through some exercises to prepare you for what we're going to do tonight. We need you centered, and with open energy fields. I don't want you walking in cold."

He set his muffin back down, and brushed the crumbs off his hands. "Well," he said. "Should we get started, then?"

It was only when he said the words that Brenda realized she'd been stalling. Where in Goddess's name was her discipline?

"Get comfortable," Brenda said, "but let your body remain open. Don't slouch, or slump. Doing that impedes the energy flow, and makes everything more difficult. Slow your breathing down. Let your palms rest upright on the table, or on your thighs, and make sure your feet are flat on the ground. Take in a deep breath and allow your spine to float up from your pelvis. Let your head rest gently on top of your spine."

She watched as he made small adjustments to his seated posture. His breathing deepened. That was good.

"Let your breath enter, expanding your abdomen and your chest, and then as you exhale, allow it to leave naturally. Don't force anything. Breathe in, then pause. Allow the rate of your exhalation to match the rate of your inhalation. Pause again. Just continue to breathe in this way."

Brenda looked around Lawrence's body. The etheric body closest to his skin took on a rosy hue as he relaxed into the process. She was amazed he didn't have any training. He took to this so easily. Throughout his bright, clear aura, she could see the coiling, snaking ropes that the coven suspected tethered him to Sharon. They were wispy and thin, but there were a lot of them.

She turned to Raquel, and raised her eyebrows in question. Raquel had her eyes trained on the young man, too. Brenda had such a hard time not calling him a boy. But he wasn't. He was around the same age as Moss, she suspected. Early twenties, filled with life and vitality.

She leaned toward Raquel and lowered her voice. "What do you think?"

"I think I'm glad the boy's a natural," her friend murmured. "I can also see those nasty cords. I'd sure like to know how they got there."

Brenda nodded and then leaned back in her chair. She stretched her arms above her head, then lowered them again. Goddess, she needed to get back to her yoga practice.

"Just keep breathing, Lawrence. I'll give you further instruction in a moment, but for now I just want you to get used to this."

She raised a hand palm up towards Raquel and then gestured from Raquel to Lawrence. An invitation for Raquel to take over.

"Lawrence?" Raquel said. "I want you to keep up what you're doing. Keep breathing. And as you listen to my voice, I want you to find your center. It's very important. And I want you to breathe into that center and as you exhale, I want you to notice the energy fields around your body, and I want you to notice what is yours and what is not yours."

As Brenda watched Lawrence, his brow furrowed in concentration, and maybe confusion. She didn't blame him. This all had to be really strange. He was getting thrown in the deep end; this morning session wasn't nearly enough to get them ready for what they were about to do, but sometimes that was how things were. Magic wasn't always convenient.

Raquel continued. "And now I want you to remember who you are. Think of who you, Lawrence, are at your core. Pay attention to the space just above the crown of your head. Imagine there is a golden crown up there. Or a globe of light. Or an open flower. Whatever feels right to you. Whatever image comes to you is fine. And I want you to feel your center, and then feel the connection your center has to that image, that symbol above your head. And as you breathe, feel the connection between the two grow stronger. And when you feel ready, when you feel like you have this connection, I want you to say out loud the words *I am*."

Brenda breathed in herself. She felt her own connection to her inner divinity. It was still there, despite everything. She give thanks to Diana and to Lucifer—the Moon and Sun—and to her ancestors, and to those who were yet to come. She gave thanks for her daily practice. And for magic. She still had some anxiety, it was true, but Raquel's words reminded her of who *she* was.

She felt the globe of light surrounding her head. She felt her aura, shimmering, moving, brighter than before. Despite the absence of the Voice, she knew that she was home. That magic was her life. That she was dedicated to the mystery of it all.

"I am," Lawrence said.

"I am," Brenda, Raquel, and Louis responded.

"I am," Lawrence said, and the other three said it with him. Three times, they uttered the sacred phrase. The phrase that acknowledged they were whole, and aware, and part of the cosmos itself.

Raquel nodded at Brenda to take over.

"Feel the breath moving through your body, all the way from the souls of your feet to the crown of your head. Now tilt your head back, and send a breath upward, blessing your crown."

He did so, and all of his energy centers snapped into place. Even the cords still snaking outward couldn't stop the force of alignment.

"And when you feel ready," Brenda said, "open your eyes."

After a long, shuddering breath, he rotated his head on his neck, and opened his eyes.

Those eyes shone with excitement, but he was trying to act all cool, picking up his coffee again and sipping at it like it was no big deal.

Brenda wished they had six months to train him for this. But if they had six months, he likely wouldn't have shown up at her door.

"How do you feel?" Raquel asked.

"Ready."

He was so brave. He probably *was* ready. But that was mostly because he didn't know what he was getting himself into. She remembered being that way. Once upon a time.

She would get herself ready too. She was a professional. A psychic, a priestess, and a witch. But that didn't mean she had to like it.

She just wanted all of this over. She just wanted to take Caroline on a proper date, get to know her, see what life was like when the coven wasn't running from crisis to crisis.

32

CAROLINE

Caroline was propped on a padded stool behind the counter of the Inner Eye. It had been an exhausting day, after an exhausting week.

Caroline had decided against going to the police to file a report, but Sydney recommended that she write everything down, just in case.

She had spent most of the day writing down everything she could remember about the abduction. Then she wrote down everything she remembered about Rafe coming at her in Salem. And then, once she finished recording that incident, she had started documenting every single other incident for the past several years. Anything that came into her head, she wrote it down. It didn't matter if it was in order. She just needed a record. Her hand was cramping up, and she was still writing.

There was too much. Some things she had barely remembered, until she started this whole process. Then the words came pouring out.

This was your marriage, she thought. It made her

stomach clench. She didn't know whether she wanted to punch something or cry.

Caroline didn't know if this twisted record was helping her or hurting her. She figured it was cleansing, at the very least.

"Get the poison out," she murmured.

She and Joshua held down the fort at the Inner Eye while the coven prepared for the ritual. His shop closed earlier than Brenda's, and he had offered to do this rather than joining the coven and Frater Louis.

"They've got enough people," he had said. "I'm happy to help Brenda out this way."

Caroline looked up from her notebook. She probably should've just been typing this all into a computer—it would have to be transferred later—but it felt more cathartic to write it all out. She liked the pressure of the pen digging into the paper, loops forming words, forming sentences. Maybe that was its own form of magic.

She set the pen down and shook out her hands, then began massaging her right hand. She'd been writing for what felt like hours.

Rubbing her eyes and forehead, she thought about going into the back room to make a cup of tea.

"There's something I still don't understand," she said, turning to Joshua. He was at the other end of the glass display counter, reading some thick tome about angels or demons or who knew what.

"What's that?" Joshua said. He put his thumb on the page to mark his place. "What don't you understand?"

"I don't understand, if the coven bound him, how did Rafe still find me?"

Joshua took an Inner Eye business card and slipped it into the book before closing with a thump.

"That's a good question. I think the coven figured Rafe had just been tracking you via your phone. They didn't know he was corded into you. You said Shani mentioned how the cords looked like your energy? My theory is that he'd been cording into you for so long, your own energy likely wrapped itself around his. It happens a lot with long-time couples who aren't careful to keep their autonomy. That thing they're doing with Lawrence tonight? At the end, if all goes well, the ritual will un-cord him from Sharon."

"The way Shani did to me."

"Right. From what you described, I think Rafe is bound up tight, and I think it's probably freaking him out. He couldn't hurt you right? In Salem?"

Caroline shook her head. Joshua was right about that. Like she'd told Brenda, Rafe hadn't gotten near her. And when she thought about it further, he couldn't even get near her *before* Michael had appeared. And wow, wasn't that bad ass? An actual archangel, coming to her rescue.

"See? So the binding itself worked, but he still feels compelled—or *felt* compelled—to track you down. Once a pattern is set, it takes a lot to break it. But hopefully he'll leave you alone from now on."

Caroline sighed and walked around the shop. She needed a break from writing. It was kind of strange that no customers were in the store. She figured evenings would be busy.

Something about the whole Rafe situation still didn't sit right with her. What Joshua said made sense, and maybe Caroline just didn't understand how magical bindings worked....

But she couldn't shake the feeling that he was still out there, waiting for her.

Bound or unbound, she could feel his fixation on her like a knife.

33

BRENDA

Brenda sat, fully clothed, toilet lid down, in Raquel's downstairs powder room, which was tucked beneath the stairs. Raquel had painted it bright turquoise and decorated it with mermaids. Raquel had an affinity for the ocean.

She was avoiding going upstairs to the ritual room. She was avoiding starting this thing.

Brenda could feel the coven waiting for her, and knew the space would be set up perfectly, and that their guests were likely wondering where the hell she was. Raquel, too. She could feel her friend broadcasting a *Get up here, girl. Right now.* She was doing her best to ignore all of it.

Finally, she sighed, rose, and washed her hands. Leaning on the white pedestal sink, Brenda stared at herself in the orange-framed mirror. Brown hair in its usual messy bun. Eyes a bit more shadowed than she wanted. Lipstick eaten off hours ago.

Tonight, she couldn't see any halo, or aura of light, or avenging angel. All she could see was a woman in early middle age, who was pissed off and didn't know what to do.

Closing her eyes, she listened for a moment. Listening

for the Guides who always showed up when she needed them. Listening for the Voice, too. Listening for anything at all that would help her navigate this convoluted mess that didn't seem to have any possible outcome that would feel righteous, or good.

If they helped Sharon get what she wanted, they would go against their tenets of not harming innocent people whenever possible. Sharon's method involved too much collateral damage. There were too many casualties en route to taking out the actual targets.

If they didn't help Sharon? Exactly the same. Innocent people would be harmed.

There was no way through without causing major harm this time, to someone.

"Diana? Lucifer? Any insight here? Any protection or liberation? Huh?"

The Gods were silent, too.

Her eyes snapped open, sparking. She felt a rush of rage. Oh yeah. Brenda was ready to go on a rampage. If only she thought it would do a damn bit of good.

Slamming up on the faucet, Brenda stuck her hands into the icy flow of water.

She was angry. Angry at the Voice for not warning her soon enough. Angry at Rafe, for harming Caroline, and returning to do so, again and again. Angry at the police and that judge, for doing Sharon and her daughter wrong.

Cold water rushed over her hands until it felt almost painful. Brenda cupped her hands, bent, and splashed the water on her face. She needed to cool down.

She was angry at Sharon's lack of training, which was wreaking havoc on people who had nothing to do with the situation.

Angry at herself. For all her training, for all the coven's

work, they shouldn't have gotten so gobsmacked by all of this.

And how, exactly, were you supposed to fix a thing you didn't even know existed? Raquel had said that to her earlier.

Brenda shut the water off. Tried to deepen her breathing. Tried to remember to open the soles of her feet and the crown of her head. She really needed to get ready for the ritual. Now.

Water dripped down her face, mascara running in dark brown rivulets over her cheeks. She grabbed a dark blue hand towel off the rack and mopped at her face.

They *had* known. She *had* known.

Everyone knew that partners abused one another all the time, and that one would often trap the other in a game of cat and mouse, until the worst happened. Everyone knew that people in power abused people they saw as having no power.

And the coven certainly knew there were issues with the Portland Police Department. That was clear enough. And oh boy, were they people in power.

The Black female judge? Well, that still came as a surprise. But the systems around her didn't.

"So, what you're going to do now, Brenda MacMillan, is get your shit together, act like the priestess you are, and go upstairs to do this thing."

34

CAROLINE

Caroline lightly ran her fingers over the display of crystals, noticing what stock was low, and what they had a lot of. There was some beautiful pyrite and labradorite. A lot of rose quartz and hematite, of course. Those were always popular. She should see if Brenda wanted any of the rarer gems, or if they just didn't sell much here. Every shop was different.

The bells on the door chimed. Caroline looked up, chilled to the core.

"Why do you keep following me?" she asked. "And how did you find me this time?"

It was Rafe, standing in the doorway, seeming spooked, and a little frightened. That was strange. Rafe never looked that way. Caroline had trouble feeling much sympathy for the man though. Her wrists and arms still ached from the handcuffs and where he had grabbed her. For the first time in her life, she felt as though she saw Rafe clearly for what he was.

A scared, cowardly little man.

"I saw the Jeep. Figured you'd be here."

"I would've thought you had learned your lesson by now," she said, a flash of anger making her feel bold. Confident.

He stepped further into the room, head swiveling as though looking for another exit. What in the hell was wrong with him?

"If you need me to, I can kick him out." That was Joshua, who moved around to the front of the counter. He stood, arms at his sides, but in a stance that telegraphed a readiness of move.

"You?" Rafe said, sneering at Joshua as he took in his fancy waistcoat and well-groomed hair. Well, that was his old self, wasn't it?

Caroline kept her distance but moved into the space between the two men.

"I don't think you have much say in this matter, Rafe," she said.

Rafe wasn't acting like himself, not at all. He stood there, clenching and unclenching his fists, hands at his sides. Not yelling. Not moving toward her.

Maybe Selene's binding was working after all.

He turned back to her, eyes haunted. "What did you do to me?"

"I might ask you the same. For the past several years. But right now? I woke up. And then I left."

"But I need you."

He sounded lost. She bet he was. She also didn't care.

"I'm not coming, Rafe." The bells jangled over the door again. Rafe whirled around. Joshua stepped forward.

And Sharon stumbled in, shrieking, clutching and tugging at her blond curly hair.

"I'm on fire I'm on fire I'm on fire!" She jerked, spun, and flailed, crashing into Rafe. He tried to get his footing, but they tumbled together and crashed into a display of stained glass medallions, sending the whole thing tilting to the floor.

They fell on top of the display, and rolled off the rack, still locked together. The sound of glass shattering cut through Rafe's grunting and Sharon's shrieking.

Sharon's voice sliced through the air. "Oh my God oh my God oh my God! Help me! Help me, please! Help me!"

Sharon rolled around on top of Rafe, who struggled and squirmed, trying to get her off of him. Glass crunched beneath their bodies.

Caroline rushed forward, unsure how to help, Joshua hot at her heels. Sharon's shrieks were deafening.

"What the hell?" Rafe bellowed.

"Shhh...shush." Joshua bent over Sharon, trying to soothe her. He reached a tentative hand toward her.

"Don't touch me! I need the angel! Angel!"

Caroline crouched down, trying to avoid kneeling in the glass. It was everywhere, shards of color strewn across the floor. She got her arms under Sharon's and helped to roll her off of Rafe. He lay flat on his back, panting, looking terrified. Good.

"Sharon?"

"I'm on fire," the woman whimpered. Her hands and face were dotted with red where they'd ground into the glass. Tears ran down her cheeks. Colored shards littered her blond curls.

"Let me help you up," Caroline said.

She looked at her husband then. Joshua had gotten him into a sitting position and was brushing the glass off of him with a towel he must have grabbed from the back room. Caroline had no idea when he could have gotten it.

"Rafe?"

He looked at her, face blank. It was funny—that was just how she felt looking at him. Blank. Just...done.

"I think you should leave now."

Rafe nodded. Joshua helped him to stand up, and brushed more glass off Rafe's clothing until Rafe waved him away. He walked toward the door, then turned, as though he were about to say something.

She shook her head at him. "Just go. If you don't, I'm filing a police report. That's not going to look good for you during the divorce proceedings."

He looked as if he was about to speak again, then nodded one more time and pushed his way out the door, bells clanging overhead. Those bells were becoming jarring.

But at least Rafe was gone. And it actually seemed as though he couldn't hurt her anymore.

Sharon whimpered, snapping Caroline's attention back. Gods, she was a mess. Glass everywhere. Blood. Plus, something bad was clearly going on inside her. Caroline felt it like a pressure on her skin.

Sharon's eyes darted back and forth, then rolled up in her head, as though she was about to faint, or go into a seizure.

"Sharon? Joshua is going to have to help me get you up, so we can get you away from this glass, okay?"

"Can't."

Caroline looked up at Joshua.

"Scoot her all the way out of the worst of the glass," he said. "Then we should try to get her on her side for now. She looks like she might seize."

Caroline did her best, bunching and scooting Sharon

over into cleared space, while Joshua flipped the sign in the door to "closed" then locked it.

He bent to help again.

"No..." Sharon croaked out. Joshua sighed.

"I'm going to get a broom," he said. "Then we'll figure out what to do."

BRENDA

"By earth, by flame, by wind, by sea. By sun, by moon, by dusk, by dark, by witch's mark!" Moss swept his arms up from quarter to quarter, then sliced them up to the ceiling, and back down to the floor, sealing the magical sphere.

Brenda felt the etheric blue flame all around them creating a portal, carving out a place between the worlds. The place where magic stalked, and words held power. The place she knew she belonged.

So stop feeling sorry for yourself, she thought. *Get your yoga-toned ass in gear.* She smiled; that last was something Raquel might say. That was what happened with best friend sometimes: their words became your words, their thoughts became your thoughts. Whenever you needed them most.

And the words were right. She did need to get herself back in hand. The Voice had thrown her, showing up the way it did. It had thrown off her practice, which she had been diligently turning up the heat on for the past year. Plus, it had thrown her emotions into a tailspin.

Brenda gazed at Raquel across the circle. She looked so strong, but Brenda knew this whole situation had to be ripping her apart. Dealing with domestic violence and rape situations was hard.

The candles flickered and flared in the center, surrounding Lawrence, who lay face up on the floor of Raquel's attic, resting on top of a doubled-over quilt. He looked nervous, and who could blame him? Frater Louis sat cross-legged at Lawrence's head, hands just hovering around the young man's temples, trying to calm him, soothe him. He was there as Lawrence's guide. But he was also there to make sure that if anything went wrong, he got Lawrence out.

Not that they expected anything to go wrong, but one never knew, did they?

Brenda stalked around the circle, feeling her coven siblings as she passed. Each had their own energetic signature, unique. Some had a scent, some had a visual tag, and others? She could simply *feel* them, warm or cold, steady or wavering. There was Cassiel's forest, Lucy's cinnamon, and Raquel's ocean waves. And Brenda? For tonight, at least, she was the wind that would sweep all things clean and clear again. She had to be, or this whole operation wasn't going to work.

She started speaking as she walked the edges of the circle, pacing around Lawrence and Louis, with the Arrow and Crescent coven holding down the edges. She let her eyes soften into that half-lidded state, allowing her to see in between the worlds. Priestess sight, it was sometimes called. The ability to simultaneously see the physical and the astral planes, and sometimes many other realms beyond and in between.

In that moment, she focused on the cords emanating from Lawrence.

They were twisting, convoluted threads, thin, delicate,

but braided like computer cables or the ropes that tied a boat to a dock. The cords pulsed, and every time they pulsed, the edges of Lawrence's skin twitched just slightly. If Brenda hadn't been in this in-between state, she probably wouldn't have even noticed.

"Lawrence?" she said.

As she looked down at him, he swallowed, Adam's apple moving beneath the skin on his throat. His head moved slightly. A nod. Okay.

"I want you to do exactly what Raquel talked you through this morning. Breathe as deeply and slowly as you can. And imagine you can keep the soles of your feet, the crown of your head, and the palms of your hands open. If you need anything? Frater Louis is right there for you. He'll be there the whole time. And if you ever need me to stop? All you have to do is say stop."

That was something they debated long and hard about. Some people in Arrow and Crescent insisted that Lawrence have an out.

"He's a civilian," Lucy had said. "He didn't take this on because he *asked* for it." Not like the coven. Not like anyone who actually trained in magic, let alone took vows.

Other coven members insisted that the stakes were high enough they had to see the process through no matter what. But in the end, Lucy had won out. Brenda was glad. The more she could diminish the harm that had already been done to Lawrence, the better.

Brenda took in a deep breath herself. That was the way all magic began, with that first inhalation of life. She smelled beeswax, and a slight tang of sweat from her own body. It had been quite a day. There was no incense burning tonight—they wanted the air is clear as possible—but layer after layer of years of incense permeated the walls and ceiling of the attic nonetheless. She could smell the faint perfume of it.

She raised her arms, the soft blue bell of her sleeves sliding down her arms.

"Guides, and Gods, and Goddesses, hear me now! Allies and ancestors, and you who are yet to come. Heed my call. Help me. And you, angelic voice, whoever you are, wherever you are, I know I've been fighting with you. But I ask you now, should you want this work to be done, please join us here. Be here now."

"Be here now," the whole coven answered in return. Lawrence took in a huge, shuddering breath. She heard Frater Louis murmuring to him, "Just keep trying to relax, son. I got you."

Brenda hoped that was true. Because what she was about to do? She had never done it before.

She wasn't even certain it *could* be done.

36

CAROLINE

"What can you see?" Caroline asked Joshua. She'd managed to get Sharon onto her side, as he'd suggested, and covered her with a soft throw blanket Joshua had found in the back room.

He'd also turned out half the lights in the shop, hoping to avoid someone looking through the window and wondering what the hell was going on.

"She's sent out cords. They're everywhere. It's a tangled mess, multiple energy cords weaving in and out around a few main, strong ropes. It almost looks as though some of them are branching off the main arteries, but I can't really tell."

"But why is she reacting this way?" Caroline asked. Sharon moaned softly, interspersed with panting and crooning some strange incantations. Magic, Caroline supposed.

This was all still so new to her. Despite the years at gem shows, she'd never encountered anything like it. And what an introduction.

"I think the energy has looped back on itself and started

affecting her. It happens a lot with magic. People think spells work one way, but they don't. There's always some sort of resonance, at the very least, or active backlash if you're not careful or clean enough."

Caroline ran her hands through her hair and sat back on her heels. She was so far out of her depth, it wasn't funny. She just hoped that whatever Brenda's coven was doing right now was helping, instead of making Sharon worse.

37

BRENDA

She needed to find the place the cords connected back to Sharon. That was the key. If she couldn't do that? Then all of this was a loss. A waste.

The coven started humming a wordless chant to help support her in the journey. The sound of their mingled voices chanting, rising and falling around her, supported her. Brenda felt as though she could catch an updraft of wind and sail on through the astral planes. There were so many cords coming out of Lawrence, and that had confused her at first. She had no idea where they went. So she chose the strongest, fattest one, figuring that would lead to Sharon.

And off she went, following it up onto the astral plane. She landed softly in the gray mist of the æthers, and looked around. The cord was still there, pulsing gently beneath her hand. But it didn't seem to lead to anything.

"What is going on?" she wondered, then turned in a circle to scope out the place.

A figure walked toward her through the mist. It looked like a classic angel, with long dark hair sweeping down onto shoulders clad in a tight white T-shirt. The figure was wearing jeans. So perhaps not so classic after all. It was androgynous, something beyond male or female.

Non-binary, she thought. Sort of like Selene. The classic thing about the angel was the sweep of large, white swan wings trailing behind. The figure was so beautiful, it took all of Brenda's strength to not fall to her knees. When the angel was but a few yards away, it stopped and held up one hand, fingers facing upward, palm out.

"Be not afraid," they said.

Brenda felt the words flow through her and around her like a warm breeze. It sounded just like the Voice in her head. Spit filled her mouth. She wasn't sure if that was from fear or excitement.

"It's you," she said.

The angel smiled, then nodded. "You've put up quite a fight," they said. "That's good, it means you're strong. And you need to be strong to do what needs to be done here. And you need to be strong for the things that are yet to come."

Oh great. Brenda felt her stomach muscles clenching with tension. Just what she needed, another harbinger of doom.

"And are you going to help me with all of this?"

"Angels are just..."

"I know, I know. Angels are just the messengers of the great all that is or something, right?"

Damn. She was off balance again. Tuning into her breath, she slowed herself down and remembered both her center and the crown above her head. Sending a breath upward, she felt all the parts of herself snap back into place.

Aligned again. Like a priestess should be. And like a person needed to be to deal with a damn angel on the astral plane.

The angel just stared at her for a moment, considering. Its eyes were almost completely pupil. If she looked closely enough, she could just barely make out the pinpricks of what looked like stars.

"Walk with me," the angel said.

She followed the angel in the gray mist. As they moved, the mist slowly turned shades of pearl, with swirling hints of yellow, gold, pink, purple. Not really purple, she decided. No. It was the barest trace of lavender, just like the sky at predawn.

The cord remained in her hand. That was interesting. Was the angel leading her toward Sharon's astral form? Brenda's hand still slid along that same, strong, twining rope, even as she followed the angel's wings, feathers lifting and rising up ahead.

"Where are you taking me?"

The angel turned their head to speak over their shoulder. "You'll find out soon enough."

Great. Cryptic as always. She was coming to understand that was just the way angels were.

The pearlescent colors shifted and brightened. As they walked on, it grew harder and harder to see the angel up ahead. Not because the mist had grown thick, but because the air was growing brighter. Too bright. All of a sudden, walking through the æthers was like walking into the sun.

Brenda's heart began to race. She found she couldn't tell she was even walking anymore. Not that one could ever be said to *walk* in the æthers, but her mind liked to pretend that she could, even though it was actually her spirit moving through space and time. But now? It felt as though her molecules were drifting, pulled towards the sun, if that's what it was. Inexorable light tugged at her. She could barely feel her own cord tethering her to her physical body down below.

Some corner of her mind hoped that her coven was taking care of her body in Raquel's attic room. And then the angel stopped.

Brenda stopped, too, blinded by the sun. And she fell to her knees, and wept for joy.

"What is this?" she whispered. "Where am I?"

I am. That was her own voice, echoing inside her. But Brenda did not recall having that thought.

The angel did not answer. The angel just looked at her with beautiful, dark, star-filled eyes.

And Brenda Knew.

"Why didn't you tell me?"

The angel tilted their head and gave a slight shrug "Every person has to figure it out for themselves."

"So..." How to even put it. "You're me?"

"I am you," they said. "But I am also the eternal. I am also the never ending. There is no separation, just the All."

"And now?"

"And now, you get to decide whether we join forever, or will remain two separate beings."

"Should I trust you?" That was a foolish question, given the Knowledge pouring into her, but she asked it anyway.

"Do you trust yourself?" the angel replied.

She did. Brenda remembered what Raquel had told her —only a week ago, but it felt like years. *"You're coming up on a new initiation,"* her friend had said. Funny, Brenda had been avoiding that, hadn't she?

She stood up again, and wiped at her face. The light was still blinding. She squinted at the angel.

"Can I take care of these cords first? Before we do the joining?" she asked.

"Things will go easier if we do this first."

So Brenda took another breath, and held out her arms, spreading them wide. She dropped the cord. It floated like an astral snake beside her, holding itself aloft.

The angel stepped forward. Brenda stepped forward, mirroring its movement.

The angel stepped forward again, its outline limned in the brightest light. Brenda narrowed her gaze, then finally closed her eyes against the light, trusting that she would sense what she needed to do, where she needed to go. She stepped forward again, arms still outstretched. There was a sense of coolness, and then warmth around her. Her skin felt abraded for an instant, and tight, as though she had a terrible sunburn. Then she began to shake. Her whole being trembled, from her center outward.

She kept her eyes screwed shut, unwilling or unable to open them. To see. So she *felt* instead. She felt her entire life. Every wrong done and offered. Every bit of harm. Every moment of generosity and grace. Every laugh. Every kiss and sigh. Every thought. Every action and failure to act. And then, with a flash of heat, and light so bright she could see it even behind her closed eyes, it was done. The edges of her skin exploded, and her throat forced out a shout.

Brenda fell to her knees once more, and then her palms smacked down on to what should have been nothingness, but what felt like wood floor beneath one hand and a soft rug under the other. There was the sudden rush of scent and sound. Beeswax candles burning down. And voices, chanting.

She opened up her eyes and saw her coven, sitting in a circle, toning, and chanting, and inhaling in staggered rounds.

There was Lawrence and Frater Louis, both of their eyes

closed. And her friend Raquel, the only one whose eyes were open, staring straight at her, and then Raquel was in motion. Rising, moving to Brenda's side. She fell into Raquel's warm embrace and began to laugh.

"What's so funny?" Raquel whispered in her ear. "And why are you back?" The coven stopped their chanting.

"I guess I'm an angel now," Brenda said. "Or, not an angel, but..." She flapped her hands around herself, as if to indicate that her aura had changed. "You know. Not just me."

Frater Louis had emerged from his reverie and looked at her keenly. "You've gotten your HGA."

Lawrence breathed on, chest rising and falling, face slack as though nothing was going on around him. As though nothing had changed.

HGA. "My Holy Guardian Angel?"

"Yes!" Frater Louis beamed. "Also known as your moment of enlightenment. You are whole now, Brenda. You've achieved what every magician desires."

"And now what?" Raquel asked, dryly. "You were supposed to be following the cords. Figuring out where they connected."

Brenda turned to her, excitement bubbling up inside her core. "That's just it. I Know now. I see exactly what to do. And we can do it all from here, from this room."

"How is that possible?" Raquel asked.

Louis replied, "Because Brenda now has the ability to see and affect anywhere. She's standing in Tiphareth, the Kabbalistic sphere smack in the center of the Tree of Life."

And then Lawrence started screaming.

38

CAROLINE

Once it seemed that Sharon was out of immediate physical danger, they'd rolled her onto her back. She was so out of it that even Joshua's hands on her shoulders didn't make her flinch.

At least she wasn't screaming anymore.

"I'm going to try to undo some of those cords."

Caroline looked at him, skeptical. "The way you described them, that seems dangerous. Isn't that like trying to diffuse a bomb without it exploding?"

She didn't know much about magic, but that seemed obvious to her.

Joshua grimaced. His hair finally looked less than perfect, and he'd taken of his fancy waistcoat and rolled up his sleeves.

"What other choice do we have?" he asked. He got up from his crouch, and moved toward the long, glass counter.

"What if we call the coven?"

Joshua rummaged, opening drawers and cabinets, scanning the shelves behind the counter, looking for supplies that would help. He held out a jar of resins.

"Throw some of that on the charcoal in the incense burner. We need to clear the space. The coven won't have their phones turned on. In order to interrupt them, we'd need to go in person. It isn't safe to leave her, for one thing, and for another, I really think we're running out of time."

She did as Joshua asked, shaking amber pebbles onto a glowing piece of charcoal, and inhaled as the scent of frankincense rose around her. Joshua slammed a cupboard door, then moved on to another.

Then she went back to Sharon's side. Caroline couldn't see that he was wrong. Sharon really looked bad. Pale, as though her life was leaching away. And terrifying as the screaming and crashing had been, this whispering and moaning seemed worse. It was as if the woman barely had ahold on her own life anymore.

Caroline rubbed at her breastbone, feeling the medal underneath her hand.

Archangel Michael, help us. Show us what to do.

Someone rattled the door, trying to open it. Then a muffled curse and the jingling of keys.

"It's Brenda!"

Oh. Thank whatever Gods or Goddesses had figured out they needed her. And thank the angels, too.

The door opened and Brenda, Raquel, and Alejandro burst in.

"Are you all okay?" Brenda asked. "I was just about to deal with the cords, when Lawrence started screaming, and the angel showed me what was happening here."

The coven members crowded around Sharon and Caroline.

"Thank the Gods," Joshua said, and joined them. "She burst in, screaming that she was on fire, crashed into Rafe and the display, and ended up like this."

"Rafe?" Alejandro asked, looking at Caroline.

"Yeah. We sent him away."

"How the fuck does he keep finding you?" Alejandro looked ready to spit.

"He saw my car. And besides, this is the neighborhood where he grabbed me before. It makes sense he would come back here."

"Did he hurt you?" That was Brenda's voice. And Brenda's scent, right next to her, arms reaching around Caroline, her warmth at Caroline's back.

"No. He can't. Not anymore."

Brenda gave her a tight squeeze before letting go.

"We need to deal with Sharon now."

"What are you going to do?" Caroline asked.

Brenda's eyes swept up and down Sharon, scanning her. Raquel held her hands around Sharon's head, doing something that seemed like it was helping. The skin on her face looked less waxy than it had five minutes before.

"Raquel?" Brenda asked.

"The main cord is strangling her heart. It's not good. I think something happened to it, and that's what made Lawrence scream."

"Because Sharon was about to die."

Cold swept through Caroline. "What do you mean? What..."

Raquel spoke again, as she traced her hands over Sharon's body, hovering two inches from her clothing. "Get me some salt water."

Joshua rushed to comply, ducking into the back room and returning swiftly, ceramic bowl in his hands.

Raquel began grabbing things Caroline couldn't see, and flicking them away with her hands. Alejandro caught them in a bowl of water.

"If Sharon had died from her own magic, it would have affected everyone she'd tied up with her. Thank the Goddess Brenda saw you all were in danger here."

Brenda took Caroline's hand. "If you're willing, we can do this work together."

Caroline pulled away. "Me? *I* don't know what I'm doing! Are you crazy?"

"You've got the protection of an angel now. And that's just what we need. Two angels, and two women, working together. That just might be the thing to see this through."

Caroline licked her lips, then rubbed her hands on her jeans. Hoo boy. How was she cold, but sweating?

Touching her Archangel Michael's medal again, she felt better. Looking into Brenda's eyes, she saw a change there. Her face was luminous. More luminous than before. And in the pupils of her eyes? Caroline could see the faint shimmering of stars.

"In for a penny..." she said. "What do I need to do?"

"Stand up," Brenda said. "And hold on."

The two women rose to their feet and clasped hands.

"Raquel, you ready?"

"Alejandro and I are good to go. Joshua? Stand guard?"

"Yes ma'am."

"Close your eyes, Caroline, and no matter what happens, keep them closed. This should be quick."

Her stomach lurched, but she did as Brenda said. She felt Brenda's hands in hers. Felt the roiling, pulsing strangeness that was Sharon, who lay beneath their clasped hands and arms.

Then she felt what could only be Michael, at her back.

She heard the ring of steel as he unsheathed his sword.

39

BRENDA

Nothing had ever felt this right. Or this clear. The moment etched itself around her, as though every sense she had was turned up a notch.

Caroline's hands in hers, so soft and strong. The scent of incense, potent, filling her nose. Almost overwhelming. The crunch of glass beneath her shoes. Distinct. Too loud. Alejandro and Raquel, strong and steady.

The angel inside her. Now part of her. She felt the light, heating up her skin from the inside out. Felt the trace of wings at her shoulder blades.

She breathed in the whole world, in one moment, on one breath.

Everything felt new. Fresh. As though she'd never really sensed any of it before. She wished she had time to take it in, but for now, there was work to do.

Brenda could feel the Arrow and Crescent coven, back in Raquel's ritual room, doing what needed to be done. It was good to have a well-trained group to put your trust in, knowing that key players could be called away in an instant and the working would still hold.

And that two workings could be done simultaneously, from a distance.

They were getting better at this world-saving business.

"Angels of all that is, Michael and the Nameless One, guide our human hands. Unravel this magic, this poison, that has its grips in this woman, Sharon, and that she has spread throughout this city, causing harm to herself and others."

Caroline adjusted her grip beneath Brenda's hands.

Brenda took a deep breath, and dropped her attention more deeply into center, showing Caroline what to do through the connection in their hands. She felt the other woman's energy deepen. Once she felt secure, Brenda allowed her own attention to broaden. She felt the Angel Michael with his sword, and the power of Raquel's ocean. She tasted Alejandro's magic, and in her mind's eye, saw the sphere Joshua built around them all, locked into the permanent protections of the Inner Eye.

Everyone played their part.

"Know this: that I, Brenda MacMillan, call upon the forces of righteousness within this city. And I call upon the power of the coming Equinox to shift the balance toward justice here."

The power built, slowly and surely, one layer at a time.

"And I call upon the winds of change. Blow through!"

Her hair began to whip around her head. Glass shards pelted her ankles. The bells above the door rang.

She hoped Caroline's eyes were still closed. She needed her now.

"Let the winds of change bring both healing and justice! Heal this woman, Sharon, of the illness rooted in her soul. Untether Lawrence, and all the others her magic has its hooks within. But do not let the need for justice die."

Her voice grew in power, building with the wind.

Sharon started moaning, louder and louder. Brenda felt her knock into her legs. She must be rolling on the ground.

Then Raquel's voice. "Be calm. You are safe here. Be calm."

Alejandro took up the chant as well. Brenda felt Sharon's panic subside.

The words filled her whole being. The wind roared through the shop, almost deafening now. Brenda gripped Caroline's hands more tightly, holding on.

"Let it be said! Let it be known! There is no healing without justice! There is no order or rebalancing while wrongs refuse to be put right! Angels! Allies! Protectors! Spirits of Portland itself! You of land and river, you of bridge and sky! Shift the balance of power. Let every woman in this city feel protection. Let every child feel safe tonight. Let everyone who is struck by their partner's hand find an end to their abuse. Let every abuser fall."

Over the wind, she heard the sound of weeping. Caroline.

Stay strong, she thought.

This was the most difficult piece of magic Brenda had ever attempted. To loose the cords without giving up the magic. To send forth healing, while not releasing accountability for harm.

The light surrounded her, infused her, overtook her. She breathed it in on the roaring wind.

:True healing always re-orders the cosmos.: The Voice. Her Voice.

Brenda nodded. She Knew now that this was true. And so, it was time.

"Michael!" she called. The archangel behind Caroline stepped forward.

"Cut these cords! Slay the dragon of sickness and abuse of power! Bring justice for the raped, abused, and beaten! Set these people free!"

His sword came down, severing every cord at once. Sharon arched her back and screamed. The cords flew off, whipped away by the power of the wind.

Brenda let go of Caroline's hands and began drawing symbols in the air. She caught up fragments of stained glass, and shaped them into one bright, glimmering sigil, fused together with her magic and her will.

"Bind those who wish to harm! Free those who need their freedom. Bind those who wish to harm! Free those who need their freedom!"

Raquel's voice joined her. Then Alejandro's. Then Joshua's. And finally, yelling, came the strongest voice of all. Caroline.

The chanting built and built around Brenda. She charged up the sigils, pouring the magic into the glass, until it was enough.

She Knew that now. More than ever before.

Then she raised her arms and felt her wings unfurl.

"As I do will! So mote it be!" Her hands, like blades, sliced down. The wind stopped.

She caught the stained glass sigil in her hands.

"It is done," she said.

And Brenda MacMillan, priestess and witch, would never be the same.

Ever again.

40

CAROLINE

Caroline gasped, her whole body rocked from the sudden cessation of the wind, the sound, and the wall of energy that had suddenly collapsed. It was all she could do to remain upright.

And to breathe. Who knew that pushing so hard against something only to have the object you were pushing against suddenly vanish would leave a person breathless?

She slowly opened her eyes, and blinked at the sight of Brenda, a gorgeous piece of stained glass in her hands, seeming to float several inches above the ground.

"Oh." That was the only sound she could push out, past her lips. She blinked again, and watched as Brenda slowly settled back down, feet flat on the floor.

"How?"

Brenda just shook her head, then walked around Sharon, whom Raquel and Joshua were slowly helping up into a seated position.

And then Caroline was encased in Brenda's arms. She could feel one hand, resting just behind her heart. The other hand must have still held the stained glass, because she couldn't feel it. But she felt Brenda's warmth, and breathed in the fresh, spring day scent of her.

"Ice cream," she murmured into the soft skin of Brenda's neck.

"Ice cream?" Brenda murmured back into her hair.

"I want some. And you smell kind of like ice cream right now. Caramel."

Brenda held her more tightly, breasts pressing softly against breasts, belly touching belly, hips supporting hips.

"I'll get you as much ice cream as you want," Brenda replied, then tilted her head back until Caroline was looking into the star-pupiled eyes. Then lips were on lips, warm, firm. Tasting of heat and light and things Caroline didn't even know how to describe. All she knew was that she wanted more.

When they finally parted, they both had stupid smiles on their faces, and Brenda's eyes were her own.

Good Gods. Caroline actually falling for this woman. Or was it some strange, trauma-induced rebound?

Shut up and enjoy it, she said to herself.

They turned then, and followed Raquel and Joshua, who had actually managed to get Sharon on her feet and were walking her into the back room, toward the round table and chairs.

"I'll put the kettle on for tea," Caroline said, "after you give me one more kiss."

Brenda obliged, then drew Caroline into another embrace. She sighed. "You feel so good. But I guess we need to deal with clean-up first, don't we?"

"We do," Caroline said. "But I want more of this, and soon. Okay?"

"You're on."

Brenda looked around the Inner Eye, at the tangled

display case pieces scattered on the floor, and the shards of glass Joshua hadn't managed to get with the broom.

Then she held up the glass in her hands. It was gorgeous. A seamless swirl of amber, red, blue, and green. No leading held the pieces together. They flowed together as though they'd come out of the fire that way.

"Magic," Brenda said, as they both looked at the glass. "It's something else."

Caroline took in a huge draft of air. The edges of her skin still vibrated, and the medal at her chest was warm to the touch. Her amethyst point hummed in a way that she could only describe as happy.

Maybe she had a chance at happiness now, too. It sure felt that way. She gave Brenda another kiss, soft and quick this time. Both a question and a promise.

Caroline looked at the swirl of glass again. This woman had made that, in an instant, and it shouldn't have been possible. This was her life now, if she chose it.

"I guess I better figure out what magic means to me."

41

BRENDA

Four days later, Equinox dawned clear and fresh.

The wind had blown through the whole city, it seemed, not just the Inner Eye. The Arrow and Crescent coven was gathered in Raquel's backyard. They'd decided on a Saturday afternoon party. After the two intense rituals they'd all been through in quick succession, no one had the heart to do more than eat some food and drink some tea in the company of friends.

Raquel's vegetable beds were just sprouting, sending up runners for sweet peas, and a variety of lettuces had taken root. They looked like they'd be ready to eat in another week.

A Japanese maple was the centerpiece of the backyard, nestled in a clearing in the middle of an otherwise ivy-choked hollow. Brenda always felt the fey lived there. It was wild and untamed, as were the corners where the compost barrel lived and the corner opposite, lorded over by a towering pine.

Daffodils added color around the fence. The coven members and their partners and friends looked like flowers themselves, all wearing different shades of purple, orange, and green. Lawrence was there, in a sky-blue T-shirt with some sort of mandala printed on the front. He was talking with Frater Louis, who had livened up his black dress shirt with a mint green pocket square.

Joshua's waistcoat was patterned all over with turquoise and yellow flowers.

Everyone was ready for spring, it seemed.

Raquel and Cassiel had taken the day off from the café to join in, and had laid out several fat teapots, all steaming under cozies, filled with six different kinds of tea. Moss and Cassiel took it in turns to run back into the kitchen to heat more water when one of the pots got low.

Tobias had made a chocolate sheet cake with fresh mint frosting. Brenda had never tasted anything like it before. She watched Caroline across the garden, talking with Sydney and her husband, Dan. Brenda liked both of them. They seemed stable, and just what Caroline needed. She was introducing them to Shani, who ran the shop down in Salem. Their laughter carried across the ivy-filled hollow in the middle of the yard.

Brenda wandered over to drop off her cake plate and grab a cup of tea. She gave Raquel a hug before choosing a cup. "Any particular tea you recommend?" she asked her friend.

"The hibiscus blend is particularly good, I think. How are things going?"

Brenda gave the "so-so" hand gesture, then took a sip of the tea. It was tart and fragrant, cut with lemongrass and rosemary.

"You know, still unsettled, but the shop is back in order, at least. Rafe seems gone for good, and the magic from the fused glass charm seems to be holding."

Raquel drank her own tea and nodded. "And that judge that came to you is setting the wheels in motion to prosecute the officers who raped Sharon's daughter?"

"Yes. And that's a good thing."

Tobias's new boyfriend, Aiden, carried a fresh pot of tea out from the kitchen. He had a stupid grin on his face, as did Tobias, who followed him out onto the small brick patio, hands filled with mugs. She supposed that Aiden would say it wasn't justice, not yet, but it was at least a step in the right direction.

"Hi Aiden," she said. He worked in a local soup kitchen and seemed really good for Tobias. They were good for one another. Lightened each other up.

"And Sharon?" Raquel asked.

"Alejandro and Aiden helped get Sharon and her daughter into a program for trauma victims and survivors," Tobias said. "But, you know. They've both had it pretty rough."

"Healing takes time," Raquel replied. Wasn't that the truth?

Brenda turned her gaze back to Caroline, whose dark sheet of hair was loose today, falling around her shoulders. She wore a crisp white shirt beneath a fuchsia sweater. Her slim hips were encased in blue jeans. It was still early days, but Caroline seemed to be bouncing back just fine.

Caroline looked up and caught her staring. Brenda's face cracked into a smile. She couldn't help herself. Caroline waved her over.

"Excuse me," she said.

"Don't let us get between you and a hot woman." Tobias laughed.

Brenda smiled, and smacked his arm. As she carried her tea through the garden to the other side of the small maple tree, Brenda reflected that this had been one of the hardest months in her life. But it was also turning into one of the best.

She slid an arm around Caroline's waist. They were only two or so inches apart in height, which meant their bodies, so far at least, were a nice fit.

And the sex was great.

Brenda noticed what she was calling The Angel Part of her—she really was going to need to come up with a better name—responded to the traces of Archangel Michael that still wrapped around Caroline like a shawl. She wondered if he would stay with Caroline long term, or move on, the way some entities did.

Her angel, though? It was there to stay. Thick or thin. Rich or poor. At least now that it was rooted in her energy field, she didn't feel the need to vomit and pass out all the time.

You can call me Sariel, the Voice said. *If you need something to call me.*

Sariel? Brenda thought. *That's your name?*

She got the sense of a shrug and a "good enough."

"Sariel," Brenda said out loud.

"What's that?" Dan, the big, bearded, sunny man towered over the group, but it was funny, he wasn't intimidating at all. Just warm, like the sun. Definitely good for Caroline to be around.

"Well..." How to put it to a civilian at a party full of witches and magic workers? "I've got this being attached to me now, I guess you could say. It's here as a helper, and it feels like an angel. It just told me its name."

Frater Louis and Lawrence walked up as she was speaking, each holding a plate of cake.

"Sariel is the angel of guidance," Frater Louis said. "So

that's a good thing."

Brenda felt Caroline's arm squeeze her waist.

It *was* a good thing. It was *all* a good thing.

For the first time in too long, Brenda realized she felt happy.

She raised her mug of hibiscus tea. "Happy Equinox, everyone!"

"Happy Equinox!" The phrase echoed through the garden.

"May balance find this city once again," Raquel said, still standing next to the tea table. "Arrow and Crescent, I'd like us to say the Equinox Prayer, all together here, now."

The coven members raised their teacups, and everyone else followed suit. Taking Raquel's lead, nine voices filled the garden.

"May light and dark, day and night, teach us what it means to softly tilt with the cosmos, balancing strength and weakness, fear and hope, love, joy, and power."

Yes. It felt good. Right.

"So mote it be," Raquel said.

"So mote it be."

Brenda wanted the balance of love, joy, and power, with all her might. She wanted the other pleasures spring brought, as well. Like the possibility of growth...and love. She turned to the gorgeous woman beside her then, and smiled.

"To spring," Brenda said, clinking her teacup to Caroline's.

"To spring," Caroline replied. And then, other people be damned, they gave each other the longest, sweetest kiss ever. It tasted of mint, chocolate, and hibiscus, and felt like a blessing.

Like just the right, new, thing.

REVIEWS

Reviews can make or break a book's success.
If you enjoyed this book, please consider telling a friend, or
leaving a short review at your favorite booksellers or on
GoodReads.
Many thanks!

Want to know what happens when Raquel's son is threatened?
Find out in By Sea

T. THORN COYLE
AUTHOR OF THE PANTHER CHRONICLES

BY SEA

THE WITCHES OF PORTLAND
BOOK FOUR

BY SEA

She looked ahead on the sun-washed shoreline and saw Zion's dark shape, playing chicken with the waves. He knew better than to turn his back on the ocean. Raquel had taught him that early on. The waves on the Oregon coast could reach up and snatch a person before they even knew what happened. Tourists got dragged out to sea at least once a summer.

You'd never see a local standing on a log, just as you'd never see a local turn her back on the sea.

It was good to see Zion having fun, laughing, and running back and forth, filled with the energy of a thirteen-year-old boy. Lately, the smile that usually graced his face had become as rare as sun during the Oregon winter. But he still wouldn't tell her what was wrong.

"*It's nothing, Mom,*" he kept insisting. Well, it was something, that was for sure. And it felt like more than just adolescent blues.

The sand was cool, and crunched under the balls of her feet as Raquel walked, sneakers in hand. She skirted the massive, uprooted trees that dotted the coastline like the corpses of fallen giants. They looked like the bones of some mythical creatures, who lived in a land far away. A land that time forgot.

Her dreadlocks tied back, she turned her face to the sun, and inhaled the brackish scent of salt water and washed-up seaweed. It soothed her heart and soul. The winter had been hard. She was so ready for Beltane and the warmer months.

Raquel hadn't been to the coast in entirely too long. But for a single parent running her own business, days off were in short supply. It didn't matter how busy her life was, though, she always reached the point where she just had to get close to the ocean. She needed her dose of salt water, sea air, and the screech of seagulls flying over the cliffs.

So today, she'd left her coven sister Cassiel in charge of the café, packed Zion into her beetle-green electric Fiat, and made the two-hour drive to Lincoln City.

Just up ahead was a five-foot-tall pyramid of driftwood. People loved to make sculptures of the sea detritus, and the park service always came along and knocked them back down again. The never ending cycling of nature, art, and government rules.

They'd been coming to this beach since Zion was five, after his dad died and Raquel needed to do things that got her away. Zion still loved the kites that flew in bright array when the wind was right. They'd already walked by the kites. Raquel could hear them flapping in the wind behind her. She inhaled, as deeply as she could, and held the breath in her lungs. Then she slowly exhaled. Goddess, her soul needed this. She watched the waves rolling in as she walked, tumbling and crashing into nothingness, until there was just a slender wash of water, snaking up onto the shore.

"Sorry I've turned my back on you lately, Mama." Raquel

said. "You are my heart, my soul. And I know it's been too long."

Yemoja. She of the oceans and the rivers. Siren of the sea. Protector of children and women. Raquel had been dedicated to Yemoja since long before she became a witch. She just hadn't known the Power's name back then.

Raquel had always been a creature of the sea. She even collected mermaids as a child, loving the strangeness of a being that was half human, half massive fish.

Raised a nominal Christian, it was only once she started studying magic—and she and Brenda had formed Arrow and Crescent Coven together—that she began to understand that the ocean had a Goddess. *Was* a Goddess. Or really, what some African peoples called an òrìṣà, a Power. And that Power had a name.

Raquel had worshiped Yemoja ever since.

Zion looked happy. Maybe she just needed to get him out of the city more often. Away from what troubled him. Of course, not every place in Oregon felt safe for a Black mother and her child. Her own mama had taught her that.

"But you can't let that stop you, girl," she murmured to the wind.

White-and-gray gulls swooped down in front of her, and began picking at the shoreline, looking for small crabs. A group of plovers ran towards the water, and then raced back. It was amazing how they moved in concert like that, almost as if they were one being. Kind of like bees, she supposed. She wondered how much individual plover consciousness there was.

Look at you, musing on the deep mysteries of bird brains, she chided herself.

Zion shrieked, and her head snapped towards him again, just in time to see the small wave that had hit him begin to recede. His pants were drenched. Well, she planned for that, hadn't she? Making him put extra pants and socks, and a T-shirt even, into his backpack, currently locked in the trunk of the car. You never knew what was going to happen on the coast.

The sun highlighted his limbs, and the shape of his beautiful head. When Zion was young, a local painter had done a portrait of him as a tarot card—The Sun. In the painting, his arms upraised, huge grin on his face, his whole body was outlined by bright golden rays. Just like today. Her sunny boy, he warmed her heart.

Raquel took in another breath and paused on the sand for a moment, turning to face her beloved ocean full-on. The sun was just at her left side, still high, but beginning to wester. She dug her feet into the sand, and dropped her shoes. She raised her own arms to the sky.

"Yemoja! Mother, ocean, water of my heart, of my spit, of my blood. Renew me, let me grow again. Watch over and protect my son, Zion. Whatever troubles his heart, let him know that his mother loves him...and guide me, please. Show me the best way to comfort him, and help him on his path. Yemoja, please bless our family. Give us the strength we need, and give me a sign that I'm on the right track. Blessed be. Ashe."

The light breeze ruffled the edges of her dreadlocks. Raquel needed renewal. Badly. She needed to not always work so hard. And lately? Maybe this was what people called a crisis of faith. She felt at odds with herself. With the coven. And with her own power.

She felt the salt of tears, pricking at the back of her eyes. She blinked them back and took in a shuddering breath. Goddess, so much emotion all of a sudden!

"Mama? Please. Ease this aching in my heart."

A lot of things made her heart ache these days. Another boy had been killed by police, and she was raising a Black son. The climate was still changing, the earth suffering. Some days, it felt as if the whole world were on fire. She needed the cooling waters to bathe her soul.

But that wasn't all.

"And Mama? If it's not too much to ask, maybe even send me someone to love, who will love me back."

There. She'd said the words out loud.

It had been so long since someone had held Raquel at night. So long since she had someone other than her coven and her friends to make her laugh.

Too long since someone had looked at her, just as a woman. Not a parent. Not a priestess. Not their boss. Maybe that was why she felt at odds with her power. She was sick of holding it all the time.

She just needed a damn break.

And the coven had been so serious these days. Their magic had taken a turn in the last year. It was a good thing, but damn, a woman could use some ease and celebration, you know?

And with the trouble Zion was in, whatever it was...? Laughter had been in short supply all around.

Raquel sighed, and pressed her fingers into the corners of her eyes. She wanted love and everything that came with it. She just didn't see how it was going to happen. When did she ever have time to meet someone? And she sure didn't have the energy to waste on those dating apps. She'd heard they were mostly for sex these days, anyway. Not that she had anything against sex, but she did okay for that on her own. She *wanted* sex. But she wanted it mixed in with the possibility of love.

"Zion!" she called across the sand.

His head whipped around, and he grinned, a broad smile filled with white teeth. He ran toward her, feet churning the sand as he went, streaks of it sticking to his wet jeans. Raquel couldn't help but smile.

"Where are your shoes?"

He pointed toward one of the big logs behind her.

"Up there. But Mama, look what I found!"

He held out his hands. In one small palm was a sand dollar, perfect and whole, untouched by the beaks of the seagulls and the ravages of being bashed against the shore. And in the other palm was a beautiful, soft-edged piece of turquoise. Sea glass.

"Oh baby, those are beautiful."

"Hold out your hand," he said.

She did, and he dropped the sea glass into her palm.

"That's for you."

"Thank you baby, I love it." She folded her son into her arms, just for a moment, looking at the ocean over his head. He smelled of the sea, and the sweat of a boy.

As always these days, Zion pulled away first. She wondered how quickly the day was coming that he wouldn't let her hug him in public at all. Soon, she bet.

"You hungry?"

"Yes!"

It was so good to see him happy.

"Let's go get some food, then. Get your shoes on."

As Zion raced to get his sneakers, Raquel turned toward the ocean once again. She held up the sea glass toward the ocean. It glowed in the light of the sun. Luminous.

She hoped this token from the ocean was a sign that good things were coming.

ACKNOWLEDGMENTS

I give thanks to the cafés of my new hometown, Portland, Oregon. All you baristas are fine human beings.

Thanks also to Leslie Claire Walker, my intrepid first reader, to Dayle Dermatis, editor extraordinaire, to Lou Harper for my covers, and to my writing buddies for getting me out of the house.

Speaking of house...thanks as always to Robert and Jonathan.

Big, grateful shout out to the members of the Sorcery Collective for spreading the word!

And last...

Thanks to all the activists and witches working your magic in the world. This series is for you.

Evolutionary Witchcraft

Kissing the Limitless

Make Magic of Your Life

Sigil Magic for Writers, Artists & Other Creatives

Crafting a Daily Practice

ABOUT THE AUTHOR

T. Thorn Coyle has been arrested at least five times. Buy them a cup of tea or a good whisky and maybe they'll tell you about it.

Author of *Steel Clan Saga*, *The Witches of Portlund*, and *The Panther Chronicles*, Thorn's multiple non-fiction books include *Sigil Magic for Writers, Artists & Other Creatives*, and *Evolutionary Witchcraft*.

Thorn's work appears in many anthologies, magazines, and collections. They have taught magical practice in nine countries, on four continents, and in twenty-five states.

An interloper to the Pacific Northwest U.S., Thorn stalks city streets, writes in cafes, loves live music, and talks to crows, squirrels, and trees.

Connect with Thorn:
www.thorncoyle.com

Made in United States
Orlando, FL
12 January 2025

57219280R00143